PROOF OF CONCEPT

ALSO BY GWYNETH JONES

PROOF OF
CONCEPT

GWYNETH
JONES

A TOM DOHERTY ASSOCIATES BOOK

NEW YORK

SCI
FIC
JON

This is a work of fiction. All of the characters, organizations, and
events portrayed in this novella are either products of the author's
imagination or are used fictitiously.

PROOF OF CONCEPT

Copyright © 2017 by Gwyneth Jones

Cover illustration by Drive Communication
Cover design by Christine Foltzer

Edited by Jonathan Strahan

A Tor.com Book
Published by Tom Doherty Associates
175 Fifth Avenue
New York, NY 10010

www.tor.com

Tor® is a registered trademark of
Macmillan Publishing Group, LLC.

ISBN 978-0-7653-8736-3 (ebook)
ISBN 978-0-7653-9144-5 (trade paperback)

First Edition: April 2017

Proof of Concept

0

Kir hadn't realized that Margrethe shared ancient history with Dan Orsted. She'd never heard the Great Popularizer mentioned (except with derision) before the so-called "Needle Voyager" idea was launched, and she'd lived with Margrethe Patel since she was a child. But now that she saw them together it was obvious, to someone who cared as much as Kir. There was deep and true feeling between them: they must have been more than colleagues! They must have been in love. Or maybe married? Till death did them part, how romantic.

Had there used to be a law that sex partners had to be married? She wasn't sure.

"And now you'll be *together again!*" cried Da Jue, the Teetip Media interviewer, with slightly mad enthusiasm, having reeled off the high points of two brilliant careers and triumphantly dug up their connection in the long ago: jovial and nervous between these celebrated senior human beings. "On this *incredibly* important project!" Jue was not human, not even the holopresence of a human. "He" was the input from a fantastically huge global audience: the statistical sum of its real-time response. (The Global Audience Mediation AI was called "it," but things like Da Jue were called "he" and "she." It didn't make sense, but Kir knew she'd better keep this in mind. Awful if she made a pronoun slip in public.) A flickering heap of number, disguised as an absurdly eager face and a bouncy body in a smart suit. He glowed and quivered, from Kir's perspective, like the patterns on his gaudy necktie. She'd taken an instant dislike to him. The soft furnishings in the interview studio glowed and quivered too, every color and texture intense and overdone.... Kir wondered what Dan and Margrethe saw. Blank walls? Hard benches? They were really upside. Kir was maintaining what she hoped was a warm, happy expression at the bottom of the Hole. She knew she was visible, looking out of a big window screen on the studio wall, but for technical reasons she had no monitor.

"But such great minds, such different goals. Are you anticipating *friction*?"

The data entity giggled at this naughty word. The global audience was getting frisky! Kir willed her smile to stay put, but she trembled. Margrethe was not patient with juniors who stepped out of line. *Don't* snap at him, she pleaded silently. *Don't* be sarcastic! They have to be on our side! Don't take risks with a *single* bad word—

"Certainly!" declared Margrethe, with a sharp, toothy

grin. "I'm looking forward to our *spats*. It'll be like being young again."

Poor Da Jue, now he was confused. And Margrethe was usually so careful with media bots. The masses are our employers, she always said. Treat them *very* gently, if you value your jobs. Her staff generally complied, though most thought it was a bad joke—

"We'll get on fine," said Dan smoothly. "It's *fun* to tease."

Da Jue relaxed. He liked fun.

"It's all the same project, Jue," Dan went on. "Always was. We've followed different pathways. Margrethe's been chasing the physics, I got into human resources. But we've always had the same secret mission, the most thrilling challenge in science—"

Margrethe and Dan turned to each other, nodding wisely and smiling warmly.

"*The Great Escape!*" Da Jue flung up his stupid fake arms, and clasped his hands for a victory shake above his shiny black, brush-cut head.

"Absolutely!" cried the celebrated scientists, in unison. "The Great Escape!"

The bot then calmed down and asked a rehearsed set of questions. Kir zoned out a little, experimenting with sneaky saccades to see how many refractions she could get from the plump fuchsia sofa cushions. She despised the Great Escape. A necessary evil, but a stinker.

But Da Jue turned his crazily intense attention on her unexpectedly, making her blink. "How about *you*, Kir? How do you feel about this? A year in total isolation! Twelve whole months, all those miles underground!"

I won't be isolated, thought Kir. There'll be almost as many warm bodies as usual on shift, not counting the sleepers, except most of them won't be scientists or support. They'll be deluded, stupid Great Escape Tourists.

"I won't be isolated," she said aloud. "I'm never alone."

The bot missed a beat; the colored shadow froze: Kir was horrified with herself. Luckily the billions decided they were unfazed. "*Come* on. You're a nice-looking young woman! Zero connectivity means no fun for you, kid!"

"Kir isn't just a pretty face," Margrethe broke in, coming to the rescue. "She's a promising PSM physicist. There's plenty of work for my teams to do, even if the Needle isn't live yet. And I think she's also looking forward to meeting our new friends!"

"Of course!" cried the bot. "All that fantastically complicated Needle stuff! Way above my head! And a crew of gorgeous new beaus for our cute junior genius. Congratulations on being part of this, Kir!"

Kir nodded in relief, trying fervently to look "cute." But the Da Jue bot hadn't finished. It lunged at her, so vividly close that she saw in its wide eyes two tiny images: a scrawny, undersized young woman with wispy blond hair and yellowish-brown skin. Looking up, out of clear dark depths. Up from caverns beneath caverns under the Giewont—

"Please. I hope you don't mind me asking. Since you mentioned him: Would it be possible to have a word with . . . Altair?"

She had to stop herself from taking a smart step backward. Now the fantastically huge global audience wanted to *grab* her. She didn't know what she was supposed to say: she hadn't been prepped for this. "You can't," she babbled. "That isn't possible—"

"Not appropriate at this time?" he suggested, helping her out with an arch wink.

"Yeah. Not appropriate right now. Altair's not, er, not ready."

Da Jue took it well, although you must never say *no*. The global audience seemed relieved, if anything.

"Well, okay. We'll need to work on that. We'll have to develop some protocols. I know everyone would love to hear from him."

The interviewer turned his smirking face to the myriads and vanished from Kir's perspective, along with Margrethe, Dan, and the whole interview studio—to be replaced by the visuals for a nonpatronizing, expertly simplified account of what this was all about, related by Da Jue. Why the isolation was so important, why the exploration of the void had been so fiercely contested. What the Needle experiment was hoping to achieve, and what success would mean. Why it was okay for the Needle to have company down there, and why the abyssal lab was an ideal locale for codirector Dan Orsted's most ambitious Long Duration Mission trial yet—

Kir would have taken the voice-over for human: it was hard to believe it was the same bot. But the global audience had many faces. She held her pose as she felt the frantic need to please and the weird concern for Dan and Margrethe's love life draining away. It was like stumbling from a centrifuge, with a sick stomach and the world still reeling. Unlike the billions out there, Kir had not been inured since birth to pumped-up Global Audience Mediation. She'd never met a media bot before Margrethe Patel's scouts picked her off the dump. Or been forced to spend any time with them since. *Never* forget where you came from, she reminded herself, refreshing the smile in determined loyalty.

You are my father and my mother. That's what people used to say, way back, when they owed someone everything, forever.

A soothing voice in her ear told her she could now

stand down. And that was it. Altair, in a sense, had survived his first public exposure. Another tricky point passed, and nothing gone wrong. Dan and Margrethe had been in no danger of screwing up, of course. Probably never been romantic soul mates, either! My father and my mother, thought Kir again.

She wasn't too sure about the father, however. Not so far. Kir did not trust people lightly.

———————

Breakout Polish cavers had been the first to discover the cavern system. They kept it quiet—what they'd been doing was seriously illegal—but word got out; their find was just too exciting. Next came the paleontologists. They went in with permission and on a very modest scale, to map the prehistoric mines the cavers had stumbled upon: older and deeper than any primitive mining yet discovered. They found the bones, a lot of bones: clear evidence that a previously unknown hominin had lived alongside early humans in the Western Tatras. Then a MegaCorps division, sensing that the Giewont Massif's *"Highest Level of Protection"* was slipping, revealed the results of an existing, mildly illegal satellite survey. Far beneath the caverns, in much more ancient rock than the crumpled layers where the flint and red ochre mines had been found, there seemed to be a void. It could be a big one, a rare and bizarre phenomenon, but the remote data wasn't conclusive. Permission was granted for a surface geophysics survey, and then, after some exciting results, a team of high-tech voidonauts was allowed underground, with a live Global Media feed. They drilled a tiny shaft in the floor of the deepest accessible cave, fed into it a rugged, specially developed, long-drop endoscope wire nicknamed Deep Throat, and guided the wire into a natural, almost vertical fault. The fault debouched, as had been hoped, into the narrow apex of the Giewont Abyss. The discovery was a global sensation: the Abyss was hailed as the deepest, largest terrestrial cavern in the world, far deeper than previous record holders, and hugely greater in volume. The MegaCorps of the West immediately started demanding full access, in the name of Science. The void's potential must be exploited!

Post Standard Model Physics, at this time, was a bundle of dazzling theories, with just-about-feasible experiments to match. The new century should have been a golden age, but since the collapse of the Orbital Toroid project, PSM (successor to Ultra-High Energy) had been wandering in the wilderness. Margrethe Patel, former director of the doomed OTP, had learned her lesson. She had her stall set up, her plans polished to a high shine, and an irresistible pitch for the global audience before any of her Giewont Abyss rivals were off the starting blocks. The protectors of the Western Tatras fought hard, but they didn't have a chance, given the societal impact of what Margrethe and Dan were offering. Margrethe got everything she asked for, including the (temporary) surface installations, the (temporary) new roads, the (temporary) high-tech infrastructure, and the blasting crews. Immense sums of money melted like wax in a flame. Every difficulty was overcome; an isolation chamber like no other was created. A closed-system lab facility, cold-sleep dorms, and living quarters ensemble was "delivered to the basement," printed and assembled around it. At last everything was ready. The Needle was installed; the human experiment could begin.

The construct known as the Needle was a volume of 4-D mapped information space. The grand plan was to shift this volume, quasi-instantaneously and with near-zero loss of integration, to some defined *elsewhere* in the local universe. The great promise, the pitch that had won the Abyss for Margrethe's team, was that in an IS shift of this kind, if everything worked, distance would be no object. Thousands of light-years could be crossed in a flash: it was the royal road to interstellar exploration. The great *problem*—as yet unsolved, when Kir survived her first Global Audience Mediator experience—was that the disturbance caused in information space by the shift swamped all measurement of the shift itself. The Needle could be made to disappear from normal Space-Time. It could be brought back, but exactly where it had been in its absence was tricky to determine. Hence the nickname. Tracking the "hyperspatial journey" was like looking for a needle in an extremely large haystack.

But all the problems were solvable. The science was as robust as Einstein, and the pristine, ancient isolation at the bottom of the Giewont Abyss was going to make things happen. Faster than light travel, the Holy Grail for this overcrowded, sinking world was really on its way!

Things weren't going too well for life on Earth, in the Population Crisis—once known as the Climate Change Crisis, but population pressures driven by climate change had long ago become the really obvious issue. By the dawn of the twenty-third century (there were other date-lines, but GAM still ran on CE, so it remained the world's common denominator) many great cities had been abandoned. All the oceans were rated dead or dying, and a frightening global percentage of agricultural land was useless. Almost the entire human population lived packed into the surviving cities, remodeled and densely stacked: the crumbling "megahives." Inside the Hives civilization survived, in a permanent state of moderate crisis. Outside them scavengers eked out short lives in the polluted "Dead Zones," or in raft clusters on the acidified oceans, while every remaining scrap of agricultural land was machine-tended, and trespassers punished with summary execution. In the West, conditions were said to be much better in the giant, seaborne Chinese megahives. Possibly the Chinese Empire's masses felt the same about the West, but hivizens didn't travel, so you couldn't be absolutely sure. Even the "One Percent," the global rich, were feeling the heat.

Most responders agreed that the Hives were a big improvement on the situation they'd replaced, but this didn't stop the masses from resenting their captivity. There was endless clamor for nonagricultural Protected Wilderness Areas, which many hivizens believed were enormous, to be opened up. When the clamor segued into violent unrest (which did happen, despite firm policing, constant surveillance, and intense Global Audience Mediation), a Land Grant Lottery was declared. The lucky winners, awarded plots of land in unspoiled locales, immediately sold the grants on the open market, usually to pay for medical treatment or to service a debt. Only the MegaCorps and the One Percent benefited, and no winners left the Hives—yet somehow the Wilderness Areas kept on shrinking, while the hopelessly polluted areas kept on growing. The good news was that global population figures, though still a problem given the world's depleted resources, were at last significantly *falling*. But nothing, as yet, was getting any better.

So everyone was hurting, and everyone was hoping for a better tomorrow, but signs of recovery were uncertain, and the people needed a dream. Conventional Space, long ago ideal for this role, was not the answer. There were colony settlements on Mars and on the Moon; there was asteroid mining; there were even outposts on the moons of Jupiter, but none of this arduous and perilous territory appealed to the hivizens (aside from the One Percent's Near Space Orbital Hotels). The Great Escape was the story they wanted to hear. Tickets out for ordinary people, to places where there was air to breathe. An unspoiled ecosystem and gravity to hold your feet down. Giant starships, mass emigration.

Dan Orsted was the colorful, tremendously optimistic figure who'd made the Great Escape concept real. His background was in Near Space Design, but he'd been to Mars twice and made enough trips to the Moon, as he joked, to earn a frequent-flyer discount. He ran his VLDMT (Very Long Duration Mission Training) programs like popular entertainment, but he insisted his project was serious, and billions of responders believed him. Why wouldn't they? Every mission had an authentic, habitable exoplanet in its sights and showcased an authentic, theoretically doable means of interstellar travel.

It was genuine science! Hivizens loved VLDMT. Dan's teams were always available: they couldn't get away! You could share their lives every moment—bitching and socializing, having group sex (on the adult-rated version), struggling with close-confinement issues, arguing about toilet paper. Margrethe Patel's pathway, in contrast, had near-zero credibility (except that Margrethe's name was spoken with reverence by a few Great Escape true believers who knew what the Needle was about). The two scripts had seemed totally incompatible. Margrethe the snooty, her Big Science past tarnished by failure, versus Dan the populist, who'd never put a foot wrong. But now it turned out they'd been on converging tracks. Margrethe had extended the hand of friendship: Dan was honored to accept her generous offer. Margrethe conceded that Dan's concept was "a positive take." Dan avowed that Margrethe's Needle science was "the real thing"—and the two tribes would be spending a year in the Hole together. In a break with tradition, and for technical reasons, this mission would not be live. But it would be a show worth waiting for, and the whole project was going to be a terrific success. Everyone was sure of that.

Kir took her blanket for company and slipped out of her

berth. Dim wall lights glowed and faded, keeping pace as she padded through the living quarters; the tokamak generator's cooling system hummed faintly. Margrethe and Dan were upside—they would arrive with the Tourists—but most of the scientists were already on-site. Behind these D-shaped doors her teammates were sleeping: Here was Karim. Then Terry and Jo, sharing a double berth, and Lilija. And that was the IS lab. (Sergey was still upside.) Malik and Laksmi, also in a double berth, and then their bosses, Vati and Big Neh: for the "Historians." Xanthe, Firefly, and Liwang for Volume Analysis, with Margrethe in charge . . . Margrethe, as usual, had called for volunteers and then made her own choices. Kir knew why *she* was here, although the baby of the IS gang, but there were puzzling names and strange omissions in this skeleton crew. Maybe it was about compatibility? Thirteen Needlers, anyway, against *forty-eight* VLDMTs (twelve officers and thirty-six crew). Not all of them active at once, but it sounded intolerable.

I'm *not* compatible. I *can't* like the Tourists, even for Margrethe's sake. Why not? Because I *hate* what they do for a living!

But who are you to judge? Would you be as angry if they were playing Cowboys and Indians for the global audience? That was an unjust war too, you know.

Huh. Heading off to kill another living world. I don't

care that there isn't a chance they're going anywhere. I hate them for wanting to.

They don't mean any harm.

The Giewont Abyss Installation was a mystery wrapped around an enigma. The enigma was the Needle in its isolation chamber, sunk into bedrock and shielded above and below by trellised lines of force. This was the experiment that was finally going to crack the deep code of Einstein's Universe (or Space-Time, or the "whole multiverse," or whatever you want to call it). And if that task took another three hundred years to complete, it would still be time gloriously well spent. . . . The *mystery* was the hollow framework set around the Needle's chamber: four sides of a square, holding living quarters, support systems, the cold-sleep dorms, and the labs. Kir knew why the scientists had to live and work in the Abyss. This was the deal Margrethe had made with the Wilderness Authority: leaving the Giewont surface, and the Abyss, as pristine as possible. She even understood the madly expensive complications that had ensued. It was the kind of irony that always happened when you turned a beautiful experimental idea into reality, just on a massive scale. But what had happened to the spartan, comfortable quarters in the original plans? Why the tiny coffin-like berths, where nobody could work or relax, and all the *stupid* great communal spaces? The oversize canteen, the games rooms, the gym, a strolling mall?

Why did we need *vegetable gardens*? We could have survived for a year without salad! We won't be able to get away from them. We'll be all messed up together, all the time—

Maybe that was the idea.

You mean Orsted's idea, and Margrethe had to say yes, because we need the money. She must have set up the deal with him long before she told us, I've realized that. It must have been the only way—

Kir had been born under the open sky. Confinement horrified her, and unlike her teammates, docile hivizens, she was lawless by nature (a trait Margrethe had never tried to erase). She'd spent hours, like a rat in a new maze, exploring the code of the Frame, and had located an inspection hatch, left soft when the assembly was complete, that could be finessed. She was on her way there now. In the chill of the outer regions, behind a row of food storage units, she found the material form of her glitch, wormed her way through the baffling, and crawled out into the void. The Giewont Abyss was not completely dark; the Frame and its cables were permanently lit. The air was dry, cool, and very still. Netted ropes of cable soared upward, twinkling with a scatter of marker lights, until they disappeared.

Kir sat down to unpeel the feet of her inner, tucking

the slippers up above her ankles. The rock felt good underfoot. She headed due south for a while, and then looked back. The Frame, half a kilometer away by her watch, was already lost and tiny, as if floating in space. She turned away from the lights and tipped her face up, imagining upside-down towers of stalactites, glassy curtains of dripped stone, like the video she'd seen of the caverns far above: fantastically magnified. But the Giewont Abyss had no features. It was an empty magma chamber, a scoured, flask-shaped hollow from which the molten rock had seeped, long ago. A black, unfathomable distance roared away from her puny light, in silent waves.

The air was good; it had been good before the lid of the jug was blasted open, but the cavern had no exits—except for the shaft that would soon be sealed. I can't get out, thought Kir with a thrilling shiver. I am alone on a sunless, inside-out, unexplored alien planet.

A hundred meters farther south she reached the break in the cavern floor she'd found on an earlier expedition. The drop wasn't deep. She lowered herself and stood on fine gray sand. It glimmered when she kicked at it with bare feet. Luminous bacteria? I'm destroying a world, she thought. Destroying ancient fossil *air*, with her every breath . . . But the Needle was safe from her intrusion, and, if truth be known, the "pristine environment" had been doomed since the moment Deep Throat breached the apex. It couldn't be helped. The level sand stretched off in either direction, like the bed of a dry river, but her visor beam couldn't discern the other shore. Maybe there wasn't one; the floor of the Abyss had yet to be mapped in detail. She set off eastward at a fast jog, pounded sand for two kilometers, and turned back, following her own footprints to her starting point. She'd met no obstacles, but there was a mysterious pressure in the empty darkness. There came a point when you couldn't dare it any further. Under the overhang of the little cliff she crouched on her heels, her blanket around her shoulders. *I'm never alone....* She still felt hot with shame about that gaffe.

The masses don't like to think about quasi-autonomous AI. WHY did I risk provoking them? I wanted attention. I didn't like standing there being ignored, like a pet animal. Hey, Da Jue! I'm a dump rat, I'm a scav. I'm the lowest form of life, but I have something very important stuck inside my skull!

Kir heaved a sigh, rubbing the permanent calluses across her brow and around her ears, from when Linda had forced her and little Vel to wear their hated face masks, far too tight, day and night.

Why at night? What good does it do when I'm asleep?

You don't stop breathing when you're asleep, said Linda's voice, harassed and tired. *The air's full of pollution, it'll wreck your lungs.*

Why don't *you* wear one?

Because I haven't *got* one. Shut up and do what you're told.

Linda and Vel, long gone, long gone, way before Margrethe's scouts turned up—(I think I once had a mother and a brother, but I can't be sure.)

Kir had let the scouts take her away, without a fight; she couldn't remember why, although she remembered being sick with fear. Because she was in trouble? She'd done something, stolen something, and Ureck was going to kill her? Or was she ill, so ill she thought she was dying? She knew she'd had a bad attack of wormy runs going on. The scouts had been disgusted at the results for their nice sanitary-sealed van. Or was it because they'd tested all the lone children they could catch, but they'd *chosen* Kir? And she liked being chosen.

The scouts were working for a special customer. They took Kir to Dr. Margrethe' s clinic, where she was cleaned up, doctored, fattened, and put through more tests. Finally Margrethe, who was not a medical doctor but something better, a chief scientist, came and told Kir she was a suitable host. She wanted to cut open Kir's skull and put a supercomputer inside. "It won't hurt," said the beautiful, incredibly ancient old lady. "It won't harm you, and it will help me in work that will benefit the world. But you must choose. Either way, you'll get an education and you'll live with me for as long as we agree. For your whole life, if that suits you: I promise."

. . . I had no idea. I said yes because it was easier, and I was sure they'd do what they liked, whatever I said. I thought I was going to be organ-farmed. Or womb-farmed. Or raped about a million times, until I died of it. Instead I got an education, and my mind felt like a universe bursting into life. I got kindness; I got so many brilliant things. You are my father and my mother, Margrethe. Fingers reached into her scanty hair, behind the headset visor, to trace the scars of wormy boils and the faint ridges where her young skull had annealed again. That's where he is, he's in there. . . .

Years later, vast ages later in her new life, she'd decided to ask Margrethe a few questions. Kir was, by medical reckoning, about thirteen. They were in Geneva, in a Sealed Enclave. The AI that Margrethe's team had built, the "quasi-autonomous artificial intelligence" implanted in Kir's brain, had been hired for some calculations by a not-too-evil MegaCorps division. Kir knew nothing about the job. When people accessed the quaai they did it remotely: she never knew it was happening. But she'd been reading stuff, and thinking about stuff that gave her the shivers. She and Margrethe were alone on the terrace outside their apartment; the poisoned lake a gleam of dark blue, through the Enclave's exclusive veils of greenery. She had asked, as if casually, why Altair was called "he."

"Because I loved my father," said Margrethe, smiling... and Kir had been disconcerted. This answer did her no good at all.

"Didn't you love your mother?"

"I loved her very much. But we were rival powers."

"Oh." Subterfuge was getting her nowhere. "Can he read my thoughts?" Kir blurted. "Is he a person?"

"No, he can't read your thoughts. Altair is contained by what we may call firewalls, and blocked from access to your personal thoughts. He can neither sense the words that you intend to speak, nor retrieve the imagery your brain invokes for ideas you don't intend to express. As for your second question, think a little harder. Tell me, what is a Turing test?"

"It's a philosophical koan," said teenage Kir, unnerved by Margrethe's stern expression, carefully repeating what she'd been taught. "Like Schrödinger's cat. It doesn't mean what people think it means. It means *you* decide if you're talking to an AI, or a person you can't see, or even if it's a sexually differentiated man or woman, by the signs you think you're getting. It's your decision, not what the AI, or the person, really is."

"So you have your answer."

The conversation had ended there, as far as Kir remembered. She'd backed off and never raised the topic again, because she'd realized that her benefactor felt guilty. Not for having kidnapped a scav kid, of course not, but for having opened a child's skull and implanted computer hardware, when the child was way too young to give informed consent. Margrethe had done nothing illegal. Nobody in Kir's new world even disapproved: scav kids had no legal status, and Kir now had a *much* better life. But guilty feelings don't listen to reason, as Kir knew from personal experience. It was better just to accept the voice she sometimes heard in her head, and show her gratitude by becoming a brilliant scientist. She would do something stunning for the Needle experiment, and Margrethe would know it had all been worthwhile.

Crouched in subterranean night, Kir fisted her eyes to make the darkness sparkle. She pressed her knuckles to her mouth, her own breath warm and moist on the backs of her fingers. But just between you and me, I'm not alone, am I?

No comment from her imaginary friend.

Kir scrambled up the miniature cliff and jogged back to the Frame, taking pleasure in the way it grew, like a floating mirage in its net of stars. She wondered if she should harden the glitchy hatch. Or report it—but decided on balance to leave its fate to chance. If I can get out, she thought, I'll explore the Abyss: for my own entertainment. If I can't I'll learn to love my miserable coffin, like a proper little hivizen. But the cables and the lights would stay in place, in case of emergencies. They would still be shining, when Kir was sealed inside the box.

If I fell down a crevasse and lost my headset (she wondered, as if she was asking someone beside her). If my watch stopped working, and I was unconscious, and nobody knew where I was, would you let me die? Rather than contact somebody to come and save me, and risk letting them know what you really are?

But the quaai was not a person, and couldn't understand speech or read thoughts, so naturally nobody answered.

1

The Tourists came down with Margrethe and Dan and other special members of the expedition. The Needle Voyager was launched with fun and ceremony for the global audience. Final speeches were made, final questions were answered, last gifts and messages delivered. The VLDMT team raced around, shouting and clowning for their fans. The casting of the cables came later and was a quieter affair. Everyone was in the canteen, their all-purpose meeting room, to see the glittering ropes withdrawn, including Sergey in his support chair. Up and up, until the last, faintest speckled shining vanished. Voices from Mission Control alternated with hissing pauses and fell silent. The LDMs had done the countdown joke at the official event, but Dan began again, orchestrating with wide arms: *Ten . . . nine . . .* And the LDMs roared with laughter when none of the Needle team joined in. "*Come on*, you guys!" shouted Dan. "Don't be shy! It's a tradition!"

"*Eight*—!" bawled Margrethe.

Seven . . . six . . . five . . . four . . .

Nobody at Mission Control could hear them. Connectivity had already been severed; the world above was out of reach.

Three ... two ... one ... zero!

The blackness of the Abyss vanished; the canteen's big screen went blue-blank. And that was it, for a whole year.

"I thought the cables would *stay*," whispered Kir to Lilija.

"Not necessary," said the other Needler absently. "There are procedures, if we need rescuing. The cables get guided and locked onto us remotely, and then the cars come down...." Lilija sighed in contentment, counting the riches of uninterrupted work that lay ahead. She had no family commitments; nobody would be lost without her. She *did* have a life, thank you. It was this, the greatest adventure in the world. And then the first live test, a rush of excitement and everybody at full stretch, in these perfect conditions. Bliss.

There was an uproar, bodies flailing: some kind of mock fight going on in the other team.

"We *have to* keep those LDMs out of the labs," said Lilija urgently. "They're the price of admission, I realize. But—!"

"We can tell them everything's radioactive in our part of the Frame."

"No, no! Don't mention danger, Kir, whatever you do!

The guys are highly trained *daredevils*!"

They burst into smothered giggles, and the knot of tussling bodies came apart. A grinning quartet of LDMs jumped up and down, flapping their arms and hooting: delighted at the Needler appreciation. Karim came over to join the two women. "Margrethe won't protect us," he muttered. "These are the masses in person. Our employers, you remember? We'll have to build our own firewalls, and *do it fast*."

———————

But the two tribes shook down together well. The VLDMT team, expansive as bullies on a playground, instantly took control of the communal spaces, and it didn't matter. The Needlers preferred their lab-habitats, anyway. Sharing the housekeeping might well have led to *friction,* but the LDMs, who never had support staff, quickly absorbed this territory as well, and the Needlers had no objection. The canteen was common ground. The LDMs sprawled over the rest of the communal spaces. The labs and the scientists' berths were sacrosanct, untouched until the Needlers themselves couldn't stand the mess—and everything was settled, without a shot being fired.

The IS analysts went back to work refining Needle search methods, getting ready for the live test in a year's time: as if nothing had changed. Kir practiced her re-fraction technique. Lilija, alongside, screened what they called the "nonspecific data." Across the room, Karim monitored the lab's Direct Cognitive working record in real time, looking out for problems, while Terry and Jo tinkered with one of their IS qubit filters. Liwang, a visitor from Volume, was borrowing an empty desk. . . . Kir's template, a childhood memory, filled the center of her field of view. Rusty water ran between rusty rocks, over mucky rainbow blocks of congealed plastic, just as it had, long ago. Upstream, out of sight, was the *abandoned Nuclear Plant*. Downstream, broken-teeth towers of the *abandoned city*. There were tiny fish in the stream, but you mustn't eat them; they were radioactive. *Abandoned, radioactive, city, Nuclear Plant*: words she didn't understand but used all the time: familiar, comfortable. The stenches of the hunting ground surrounded her, the murky sky was hot on her back, the hated face mask chafed. Feelings, things, hurts, unassociated recall cascaded through the myriad dimensions of this ambered moment, as Kir focused and refocused, in pursuit of another tiny increment of integration. *Uncertainty*—an expression she had heard used very carelessly at the "launch"—had nothing to do with the shift. It was all about precision. If Kir could track every live synapse in the information state of a moment of awareness (a staggering operation), she'd have reached "integrated definition": an important technical term. If they could do that for the Volume, in Information Space, the Needle would no longer be lost in that haystack. It would be going where it was sent, returning to its origin; and the journey verifiable.

They weren't there yet, but they were on their way—

There was a dearth of visible high-tech in this cutting-edge PSM lab—apart from the wireless Direct Cognitive skullcaps, which didn't look like much, if you didn't know. Kir stared at pictures that only she could see, a sketchbook and colored crayons her only aids. Karim tapped occasionally at a basic manual calculator. Lilija preferred an augmented reality, mediated by her DC cap, but also used graph paper and map pens. Terry and Jo had a toy percussion set, a chiming array of child-size gongs, xylophones, cymbals.... My scav family, she thought (intense mental effort, like a constant sense of danger, buffered and soothed by the familiar presences). Karim's our weatherman, sitting up on a big rock watching for ominous clouds. Lilija's the dust bunny, sifting dried-out stinky muck. She'll find gold. Terry and Jo are our "toolers," artisans of odds and ends: they earn their share. And Liwang's in here prospecting, looking for new hunting grounds for his own guys (because nothing lasts). That's why he's always mooching around, snooping.

Sergey, the IS Analysis boss, disabled by degenerative brain disease, was one of the puzzling names on the roster. He wasn't in the lab today. He'd sent his paybot, right now curled up on the workbench at Kir's elbow, to keep an eye on them. Sensing her attention, it cocked an ear and winked. Sergey is our god, she decided. Immobile, prophetic. Every scav tribe has a god. Or in real life, maybe he's a closet VLDMT fan? Maybe he begged to be allowed to come, to spend time with the glorious gang? Kir sniggered, and Lilija looked over with a wrinkle-nosed frown. "Tell you later," muttered Kir. But she wouldn't. If you thought of something that would amuse the chief, you hoarded it.

Altair is more than a god. He's the air we breathe. I'm only here because he lives in my head, and I don't mind. It's a massive privilege—

A tiny fish hung by a pseudo-rock in a poisoned stream. *How does it stay there, when the water's moving?* Kir the baby-scav couldn't make it out, and suddenly it—no, but something happened. Something had been poised, for an instant—

Altair, are you *messing* with me?

She glanced around, and was relieved. Nobody seemed to have noticed her startled movement. Not a single isolation expert had come down. That was another puzzle, until you thought about it. They'd have had nothing to do. Even when the Needle was live, monitoring its chamber wouldn't involve hard hats and boots. Everything was handled remotely.

———

The LDMs, in close-up, were nothing like the wobble-bellied, spindle-limbed "normal guys and dolls" in their publicity (Kir hadn't seen the actual show). They had the same names and faces, and physical disability clearly wasn't a veto, but they were limber, lean, and toned. They aced the housekeeping: instant experts at wrangling the Frame's domestic mech and tech. Their off-duty behavior, however, was as obnoxious as Kir had feared. They were loud, they were inconsiderate, and when they weren't tending the Frame or eating they had an *amazing* tolerance for slobbing around, in their eye-hurting live-feed overalls, doing *nothing*. Boredom would never find a purchase in their empty heads. Two weeks into the year of isolation, one of them brought his dinner tray to the canteen table where Kir was eating alone. He plonked it, folded his sleek, muscled arms, and sat back, grinning.

"Ask me anything, crewmate!"

I was *not* looking at you, thought Kir. My eyes may have happened to pass over you, a couple of times, but it meant nothing.

"Why do you all look so different?" she said. "From on the show. Are you imposters?"

"Aw, you're a *fan!* That's so cute. Nah, nah. It's a conflict of objectives. Don't tell me you guys don't have those. We have to be one way to fit with Dan's *I'm serious* complex, and another way to keep GAM happy. Global Audience Mediator—don't tell me you guys don't have issues with GAM, everybody does! It's dirty but it's cool."

"I'm not a fan. I just wondered. Which is the real you, anyway?"

He roared with laughter. "No conflict! Perfect slob mind in perfect jock body! I'm Bill, chief engineer." Grinning hugely, he popped his big mitt across the table and grabbed her right hand, which vanished in his grip. "I fix things. Well, you know. I politely ask the software to fix things. You're Kir, the infant wonder. Are you always going to be that size?"

Kir withdrew as far as his grasp would let her, and Bill dropped her hand, mugging clownish disappointment. "Uh, so it's not me? Well, okay. You must want Ben! I'll call him over?"

"I'm sorry. Who's Ben? I don't know what you're talking about."

"Okay, okay. No neeze to freeze! Ben's first officer for this rote. I'm genuinely called Bill; Ben's not called *Ben,* but we look alike. We jump around like crazy puppets, and he's a Brit, so the Brits call us the 'Flowerpot Men,' it's a Brit joke; and now you know the whole story!"

"Thanks," said Kir, grabbing her tray and scraping her chair back, intent on a swift exit. "Really pleased to have—"

"I'd better say, about Altair." Bill shook his head, stuck out his lower lip, and puffed a breath. "Whew. You poor kid. The human server-farm. You know what? If I *could* leave this galaxy, I would! It sucks, living in a world where things like that can happen to a defenseless child."

"At least there are no more wars," said Kir. "I'm not a server-farm. I'm wetware. Altair is a quantum computer; my brain supplies his life support. It isn't creepy, it's fine. If he wasn't hosted by a living human brain he'd be much more expensive and far too hot to run—"

Bill rolled his large dark eyes. "Augh, *he.* I hate that! That *anthropomorphizing* they do! They stuck this flesh-eating—okay, calorie-gobbling—computer into your head, shortening your life, which has got to happen, you must know that. Then they give it a name and try to make it sound like a guardian angel—" He jabbed a hand at his open mouth, miming fingers-down-throat, a favorite LDM insult gesture. "Okay, now you're offended. Kir, you have your script, what you have to say. I understand. I'm in that bind too. I just wanted you to know—"

"You want a ticket on the first starship?" snapped Kir, with all the venom she could muster. "Good luck. I hope you can last that long. Me, I have the more realistic goal of wanting to learn, and maybe help the only world we have to get better. Altair is *my* ticket. And by the way, *anthropo*morphic is a sexist term, which is a bad word, Bill the Crowd-Sourced, so you'd better watch your mouth!"

She sped to the counters, dumped everything including her uneaten dinner into the right slots, and stormed off.

"*Spats,*" said Bill, mugging acute embarrassment. "You heard what the boss lady said. Spats are fun! She loves me, really."

Everyone hurriedly went back to chatting and eating, ostentatiously tactful.

Kir knew her access to the Abyss was still open and didn't resist when her feet took her in the lawless direction. Don't take it personally, she told herself. It's the LDM ethic. Saying outrageous things and meaning nothing. It's a GAM thing. Crude, fake, freedom of speech for people who have none. Like a puppet on a string. . . . She crawled out into the dark. No longer a Hole, now, but a bag with the neck drawn tight. No headset, no blanket, but she had her watch, and the Frame was still lit, although its netted stars were gone. It only takes one fool (that's Bill) to rush in and tell you the truth, and you fall apart. . . . She reached the break in the cavern floor without faltering, dropped to the sand, and huddled under the overhang. Altair is the price of my admission. I *know* all that. That's not the problem, it's *Margrethe*.

Kir—

I don't understand why she brought the LDMs in. To buy us time? But next year the starship troopers will be gone, we'll be forgotten, and we'll still desperately need what she calls "the miracle of financial support" for years and years. *Why* is she doing Dan Orsted a favor? He's everything she hates. A Tourist, a spoiler of living worlds!

Kir, I need to talk to you—

Oh, the sock puppet's sock puppet. Just what I needed. Shut up and go away, imaginary friend.

Kir? Is something wrong?

Nothing. A stupid arrogant LDM called Bill came over to my table. As if he had a right, as if I'd been *flirting* with him, and he kindly told me I'm a sock puppet. I don't exist; I'm just a clot of data, pretending to be a real person. A 'server-farm' was the actual term. But I don't care about that. What I care about is that Margrethe, who is my idol, is on a path that doesn't make sense.

Oh, I see. This Bill thought you were interested in him. Was he right? Were you interested?

I'd noticed him, okay. It doesn't matter. He told me I'm disgusting. And ridiculously small.

He was probably nervous. Kir, I need you to do something. This is very important, or I wouldn't ask—

A shiver of amazement, fear, and even panic, suddenly crisped Kir's nape and ran down her spine. He was calling her Kir! The voice in her head had never, *ever* used her name before. Or asked her to do something. She sat up, staring around. Nothing to be seen, of course.

Who's talking?

It's me, Altair.

Really? I hope you can prove it, and I DON'T KNOW HOW YOU'LL MANAGE THAT! I'll have to tell someone and get medication for these symptoms. I'll have to be shipped out. The experiment will lose its quantum computer! We'll be dead meat! So TRY HARD!

No need to shout. Close your eyes, turn your head, look at me—

She closed her eyes, anger and fright overwhelmed by sheer curiosity. The weightless night of the Giewont Abyss was replaced by a nameless shade of dense opacity. She could feel someone beside her. She turned her head, eyes still closed, and there he was, printed on the absence of light. A seated figure, in the same pose as herself. But taller, different in build, and his skull was gleaming smooth. He wasn't looking at her; he looked straight ahead, stiffly, as if he was feeling nervous—

Is that *you*? Is that what you look like?

I don't know, I can't see what you're seeing. An artist's impression and you are the artist. Kir, please listen—

"Go away!" she shrieked. "Leave me alone! I can't be doing with this!"

Okay. Badly misjudged. One of us had better stay calm. Let me think, let me think—

GO AWAY!

Got it. Let's go and see Sergey. You trust Sergey, don't you?

Kir would have refused, but it sounded like such a good idea. Plus she was angry, and scared: but also fascinated—

———————

Sergey had a triple berth to accommodate his support system. Luckily he wasn't in bed yet. He sat in his chair, against a backdrop of gleaming machinery. His paybot twirled on his armtable and wagged its tail in welcome. Sergey's eyes, still able to smile and shine in his distorted face, greeted Kir warmly. She remembered she'd been going to tease him about being an LDM fan—

"Hiya, Li'l Bit," said Sergey's *nice* voice, kindly as his eyes. "What brings you? I'm not complaining, but it's my bedtime. I was about to summon my valet and retire." He had other voices. He had a fine, dandy hologram-self, progressed from the young Sergey before he was struck down, but he only deployed it for "company." He preferred to use his paybot for remote presence, in normal life.

"I've got a problem," muttered Kir, hanging her head. "I can't tell Margrethe, so someone advised me to tell you."

"Am I sworn to secrecy?"

"*Obviously*. But I know what you're like. If you blab, I won't hold it against you."

"So, spit it out?"

"One of the LDMs said I was a server-farm. They are such ignorant slobs, and *I can't understand* why they're here. It's a sellout."

"Hmm. You think Margrethe sold us out? That's very *direct*, Kir. Not like you at all!"

"Don't laugh at me, it isn't funny. I'm not coping, and the year's just begun; and I *can't* agree with this LDM stunt."

Sergey looked at her quietly. "Is that all?"

"I think so."

"Then I'll try to help. We should be holding hands; it's time for an intimate confidence." The hand that appeared and took hers was as immaterial as his hologram-self, but miraculously convincing, warm and flexible as flesh. "Margrethe wanted to host Altair. You know that, don't you? None of us contested her right. We were a team, and standing on the heads of generations of minds behind us, but Margrethe had made the difference. It couldn't be done. None of us was quite clever enough for the partnership, and we needed a child, anyway. So Margrethe went looking, and she found you. You know about the other scav kids?"

"Yeah, yeah. They all got an education and a future, but I'm the one that typed right. The suitable host."

"My story doesn't make you feel better?"

"I've heard it too often. Sergey, I love Margrethe more than anything in the world, but—"

"But she's a driven, ruthless woman, and tonight, suddenly, you feel she's hurt *you*, personally."

Kir hesitated, and nodded. The virtual-prosthetic hand tightened its grip. "She thinks of you as her successor, you know."

"Dirt," muttered Kir.

Sergey chuckled. "Possibly, dirt. Full many a rose is born to seem a budding genius at twenty-two and fade into mediocrity before thirty. I was one, as you know. . . . But you're not doing badly. You're very healthy, you will live long. You might see the promised land, Kir."

"Is he a person?"

Sergey laughed. "Ha! We're back in Darwinian-Descartes world, are we? Every being that isn't human flesh and blood is dead automata? Where does that leave me, Kir? What about my poor paybot? I don't *know* what his state of being is; the question is too subtle for me. But I call this fellow 'Gromit'—" He deployed another hand and patted the paybot's casing. "And I love him dearly. *Is Altair a person?* My advice to you, Kir, is you should consider all the angles before you announce your own answer to that question."

"Okay. I think I get it."

She hadn't been able to face Sergey when she was blurting out her doubts. She looked up at last, thinking she'd see friendly mockery, or cheery malice: something *Sergey*, anyway. But the living eyes in his slack face were just very tired, and unusually somber.

"I'm sorry. I'll go now. I'm a brat for keeping you up."

"Don't worry, I'm fine. I'll always be here for you, Li'l Bit. I promise. Good night."

Out in the passage she leaned against the wall and folded her arms, processing what she'd been told. Typical Sergey, he answered a different question. Probably he couldn't believe that Kir was really doubting Margrethe's judgment. And probably he was right; "server-farm" had stung. But she'd never thought before about *Altair* being helpless. His cruel fate, if he was truly conscious, had never crossed her mind. . . .

I'm sorry, she said, without speaking aloud, or looking at the person beside her, because she knew she'd see nothing. I had a bad day. I got a false positive in the lab, and that never happens to me. I'm too careful. . . . And Bill upset me. What was the urgent thing?

No response. Kir sighed, but felt relieved. She had more than enough to deal with, without Altair suddenly being real, and needy—

———————

Kir collected her breakfast from the dispensers the next morning and ate alone in the lab. At lunch she braved the canteen. There was a noisy group of LDM crew-persons (known as "crewbies") but no Bill. She sat at an empty table and began to eat, rather disconsolately. Suddenly he appeared, coming through the doors with another LDM so like him—although Bill was dark, and his friend was rather light-skinned—it had to be "Ben." Ben joined the crewbies. Bill brought his tray to Kir's table and sat down a cautious distance away. From the corner of her eye she saw him push something along the tabletop toward her. It was a white paper flower: a feathery, intricate origami lily.

"Sorry," he muttered.

"I'm sorry too."

Margrethe and Dan came into the canteen, looking solemn. They went straight to the raised stage under the big screen, at the other end of the room from the counters. Everyone shut up, and the silence was deafening. What was going on?

"I have sad news," said Margrethe steadily. "My dear friend and longtime colleague, one of the most brilliant physicists of his generation, Sergey Pillement, died in his sleep last night. I've just left his room. I know he will be mourned, but in a real sense—"

Tears welled from Margrethe's eyes, and Dan took over. "He was a great man. Courageous, fearless, indomitable—"

A voice rose, bewildered: one of the LDM crewbies. "Do we have protocol for this? Does it mean we abort the mission?"

"Certainly not," snapped Margrethe. "He would hate that. We will celebrate Sergey's life, *joyfully*, and we will go on—"

"*Ouch*," breathed Bill as Dan started listing Sergey's honors. "I knew he was a degenerative brain disease victim, from when he was a kid, wow, over a century ago, but I thought he was *stable*. What do they mean, he just *died*? Wasn't he monitored? Did nobody try to resuscitate?"

"Not Sergey," whispered Kir. "He's been DNR for years, and he looked after himself. Please shut up, Bill. He was my friend."

2

Sergey's family attended the memorial service in holopresence: physical quarantine was not breached. The great man's remains would stay in the Abyss, in cold storage, until the end of the joint mission. This provision had been agreed in advance, apparently. Sergey in his support chair, looking just as always, delivered his own eulogy address, with relish: praising himself extravagantly, cracking jokes. Insisting that the Needle Voyager mission must continue and wishing them well. The LDMs were a little bewildered by this posthumous performance. The Needlers were uplifted.

"A hard act to follow," said Margrethe, taking the podium. "He always was! Bear with me as I make the attempt: I will be brief. Sergey Pillement followed no specific religious faith. But he was, and I take confidence and say *he is*, a Believer. He believed in Life. He believed in Mind, and he served those two great principles, or great Beings, with all his heart and soul. He bore the inflictions of a devastating disease with courage (and humor!) his entire adult life, and by sheer stubbornness—if nothing nobler—survived for many decades, making enormous contributions to science. When I asked him to be part of this experiment, of course we discussed the risks. But Sergey managed his own clinical situation, with medical AI oversight, exclusively. I now realize he may have known that irretrievable systems failure was closer than it seemed and kept it to himself. If so, I forgive him. I know what this mission meant to him, and I'm still very glad he was with us. He died as he had lived, serving the future our world so desperately needs, to his last breath. We will miss him, and mourn him, but let me remind you: We have not *lost* his leadership, his inspiration, or his knowledge. Sergey was an uploader, as many of you know. He had been transferring his life-experience, and his knowledge, to permanent storage for a long time—"

Kir couldn't hold back the tears. Sergey, who mocked all sentiment, had held her hand last night, and told her *I'll always be here.* She'd thought he was teasing: He had known he was dying. He'd been saying good-bye.

The death was not rated as an emergency, or even a tragedy, but it did make people think. There were other fragile eminent seniors on the Needler team. Had they *all* signed secret contracts, agreeing their bodies could be kept on ice? Should the medical status of all post-lifespan Voyagers now be made public? "Okay, Sergey was one of a kind, and he was terminal," said Bill, airing LDM concerns with Kir in the canteen. "We get that he was a pre-pared death, fine: but look at Margrethe. She's the boss, and she's *ancient*. What if she has a health crisis?"

"And there's her codirector," countered Kir, bristling up at the criticism. "Dan Orsted is Margrethe's exact con-temporary."

"Yeah, but Dan's hale and hearty. Check it out, he posts his stats. None of the scientists do that. Hey, the guys are wondering, and I thought I should share, don't stress! It's not just about nonpremature death for the oldsters. What if we get overwhelmed by a devastating virus?"

A herd of zebras thundered across his torso, streaming with an affliction of starlings in flight, and on collision course with the gleaming blue hammerheads that raced over the chief engineer patch on his upper arm. Swarms of bees whizzed furiously around his thighs. Kir shook her head, wincing. Thankfully, sound effects were banned in the canteen. How many extinct species can one LDM hold?

"What if you had a critical health problem on a normal VLDMT program?"

"It doesn't happen, or if it does it's staged, not real. Tell no one! But if it *did*, we're not out of all contact with the real world!"

Kir sighed. "No. You're just pretending. It's the way

it is, Bill. Our senior scientists are here because the Giewont experiment is important to us, and the hard quarantine was Dan's idea, I seem to remember. If there was a real emergency, we'd abort. But there isn't."

"Here's hoping. Ten months and three weeks to go."

The LDMs quickly recovered their bounce. They weren't inclined to worry too much about the prepared death of an old sick person, or to stress over hypothetical disasters. The Needlers mourned. The IS analysts were distraught, until Sergey's paybot reappeared in the lab, curled up in its usual place. Nobody would admit to having kidnapped Gromit from Sergey's sealed berth, but everyone was comforted.

Kir hadn't forgotten that Altair wanted to tell her something, but she didn't hear the voice in her head, and her mind was on other things. Two weeks after the memorial service there was a night when she couldn't sleep. As restless as if her brain were itching, she decided to check the hatch. It was still soft, still easy to finesse. She met nobody on her way to the secret exit: lights out was strict on the Needle Voyager, for health reasons. Usually they were pretending to adapt to the alien cycles of a target planet—but the rule had not been relaxed, they just kept to the hours of light and darkness far above, on the Giewont. Once she was out in the void she decided to head north, and then started walking in a spiral, after half a kilometer without incident. For a while longer nothing entered her moving envelope of light. Then a ghost appeared, a black oval, spookily alive, swimming in midair! As she approached the illusion shifted, becoming a spreading blot on the rocky floor. Circular depression, said her watch. Remarkably regular, mean diameter of six meters, mean depth of ten centimeters. A momentous find! A wild animal of the Abyss! Kir groped for a pebble, but there were no pebbles, not a grain of grit. I'd better just jump, she decided, and took a flying leap—

An instant of absolute *nothingness*.

The floor of the depression hit the soles of her bare feet with a smack that made her stagger and land on her bum.

What did you do that for? You could have snapped your ankles!

Adrenaline surged in her blood. I knew it was just a puddle. . . . So you're back?

Never been away. I'm sorry about Sergey.

I'm sorry too. Did you know? I mean, that he was dying?

It's not something I'd understand. Kir, remember I wanted you to do something?

I hadn't forgotten. What is it?

I need you to go to Margrethe's berth and review some references.

Kir wrapped her arms around her knees. She wondered for a moment if she was asleep and dreaming. I don't get it. If Margrethe wants me to go delving in her antique paper mountains, why doesn't she ask me?

I don't know.

I'll have to think about it. I'm going back indoors now. Leave it with me.

Thoroughly intrigued, Kir studied the problem she'd been set. What should she do? If Altair was a real person (and Sergey hadn't left much room for doubt!), then maybe he was bored. Maybe getting Kir to look at offline documents was the quaai's idea of excitement. Naughty fun. But what if the voice she heard *wasn't* "Altair"? What if Kir was having delusions? Or what if Margrethe had chosen this roundabout way to find out what was going on between the quaai and his host? But this last seemed unlikely, and if she was honest, Kir shrank from asking her mentor. There was too much love and guilt involved: too many years of silence. They never talked about Kir being Altair's host. It was like a family secret: never mentioned, always there.

In the end she decided to do what Altair asked. It couldn't be dangerous. Altair was a person, fine: but there must be limits. He couldn't be fully independent, and he surely couldn't decide to do harm. If the voice in her head started telling her to falsify data, dump noxious substances in those stupid salad bowls, or run around slashing tasteless LDM jumpsuits, that would be the time to report herself sick.

She invaded Margrethe's berth the next morning, when the codirector was in a physical meeting with Dan Orsted and the other seniors. She had no trouble getting in; she'd always had the run of Margrethe's quarters. The berth was a double, with a cot and a capsule bathroom squeezed into one corner. The rest of the space looked the way Margrethe's cluttered office had always looked, wherever it found itself. The antique framed photographs on the desk, the shabby life-souvenirs scattered about: nothing of value, but hallowed by time. And then the books, the papers, the boxes. Shelves and *shelves* of printed books. Stacks and *stacks* of overflow, piled in tottering towers—

"Why," muttered Kir. "Why, why, why does she do it?" In the Hives an offline archive was seriously illegal: everything had to be open to inspection. Margrethe's chaotic library was protected by her chief scientist status, but it was still a grumbling intervention risk, and she just didn't care. Kir shook her head, breathing the air of home, the home she'd shared for so long. Margrethe was lawless too—she had the pointless defiance gene—or they could never have been such good friends.

Altair? Here we are. What do you need?

I'll direct you. You locate the data, I'll do the reading. It will go straight to my workspace. This will seem strange—

This already seems strange. I warn you, if Margrethe turns up and asks me what I'm doing, I'm going to tell her it was your idea.

The quaai made no response to this quip.

Maybe the secret of Margrethe's immunity was that most of her treasured junk wasn't really offline. It was freely available *somewhere*. But there were exceptions, and hunting them down was a game Kir loved. She'd been Margrethe's human paybot for years: happy to spend hours exploring the rats' nest. Tracking down a chapter in a printed book with tatter-edged pages; combing fragile printouts for a single crucial result. Altair's search presented no challenges, and only brief glimpses of past feats of discovery (the lost Toroid Project Asteroid Cloak Proposal. That controversial hyperspace experiment, never published, surviving in a bizarre smartplastique permaformat. An early Needle data analysis, in its uncensored, offline form . . .). She got through the list as quickly as possible, constantly peeking over her shoulder, sure that Margrethe was about to appear. Find a book, track down a specified chapter. See nothing. Locate an article in one of the floor stacks, run eyes over it. See nothing. It was a strange, irritating feeling. A selective, brief, but total blindness.

We're done, said Altair at last. *You won't have access to the data, sorry. You'd have to finesse the firewalls to see anything in my workspace. I know that wouldn't stop you, technically: but I'm sure you won't! Let's go.*

It's got to be okay, thought Kir, bemused. I'll ask Margrethe. Why shouldn't I? She'll know all about this, and she'll explain—

———

Kir had no intention of tampering with the firewalls in her head: but there were other ways. She had title pages, abstracts, chapter headings, and dates; and of course she was curious. She made the reasonable assumption that this was somehow to do with the Needle, invented some filters, and set her watch's modest, conventional computing power to work, just to see what happened. To her great surprise, something popped out of the data at once. An association, clear as daylight, between the metadata for Altair's list and Karim's working record on the day before Sergey died . . . Mystified, and intrigued, Kir studied Karim's record. She soon found her own false positive: noted in the traditional form, an ancient scrap of nonfunctional code: ~~Wow~~. Karim had made nothing of it. False positives aren't dangerous, they're just false. But Kir now had other evidence, and she began to get excited—

Long ago, in Standard Model days, scientists had assigned quirky names—*up, down, charm, strange, top, bottom*—to the particles known as quarks, regarded as the building blocks of all matter. The equivalent terms for information space, the four vectors (c, d, m, d), had been named in the same way, *almost* purely for nostalgia's sake. They were called cruelty, drama, meaning, and dissension. Kir took all the cruelty, drama, meaning, and dissension that her watch could handle from the work of the three labs. She refined her filters and ran the probe again, and the result just got stronger. She'd found a hint, and more than a hint, of something truly thrilling.

She remembered that Sergey had told her *she might see the promised land*.

She had dinner with Bill in the canteen and returned to Margrethe's berth for their "evening chat"—the quiet hour Margrethe had saved for Kir, whenever they could both make it, for all their years together. It wasn't always fun. There'd been times when Kir had approached a "chat" with dread—even if Margrethe was in holopresence, or looking out of a screen, the safe distance of an orbital away. But she'd never faced her mentor with such a complex burst of feelings in her heart as on this evening under the Giewont. If she'd been younger she might have blurted out her discovery, straightaway. Grown up, and not quite certain of her ground, she waited for an opening. It didn't come.

Margrethe sat beside her desk, elegant, mellow, and smiling, her trademark pure-white shift and trousers gleaming under the natural-light lamps, the habitual high-collared black jacket slung around her shoulders. She reported that the excruciating live-feed overalls had been discussed at her morning meeting, but Dan couldn't grasp the offense that the Needlers felt.

"He said his LDMs like to celebrate the natural world. He asked us, wasn't that a positive thing." Margrethe laughed, shaking her head wryly, the lines at the corners of her beautiful dark eyes crinkling.

"They could celebrate the wildlife of the Giewont Abyss," growled Kir. "Our local nature reserve. That would be acceptable."

"Well, you can tell people we're working on it. But what about *you*, Kir, and your gorgeous beau? Has he asked you out yet?"

Kir grinned. "Not so far. I don't even know if they date. They might be saving themselves for the aliens."

"You should make the first move. And what about Lilija? Can't you find her an LDM sweetheart? She works too hard, that young woman—"

Lilija was fifty, and didn't appreciate being called "young." She and Margrethe had a lot of respect for each other, but they were sparring partners, always trying each other's boundaries. Maybe they were rival powers.

Kir had once plotted to dress exactly like Margrethe, when she was older. To move like Margrethe, to laugh like that, to inherit Margrethe's elegance and *constancy*. She'd outgrown the impulse. Her own no-nonsense dress code—drab trousers and tunic, a colored inner peeking at wrist and throat—was not homage; it was her own taste. Never did get used to having a choice of clothes. But you are still my maker, she thought. My father and my mother. So I won't say a word. If I'm right, you'll be making an announcement soon. I'll wait for that.

She could think of good reasons why Margrethe was keeping quiet.

In her berth (illicitly working after lights-out), she went over it all again. The watch was a limited tool, and things that looked brilliantly right turned out to be wrong all the time: but everything seemed to stand up. There was a vital milestone, known as "Proof of Concept," that hadn't been reached when they were setting up the Giewont deal: a fact that had been rather riskily obscured from their backers. Kir's results were telling her there was no longer a problem. . . . Even better, there'd never really *been* a problem. From what she could see, the clinching results must have been achieved, waiting to be found in unanalyzed data, before the deal was signed. So there was no harm done, just a potential embarrassment avoided. Typical Margrethe, daring and reliable! Certain before anybody else: always right when it mattered.

But Proof of Concept was an incredible boost for the live test! And at last Kir knew why the LDM stunt was worthwhile! A year's funding, courtesy of the insufferable Dan Orsted, was all they needed. After a successful live test, first time of trying, the Needle would be beating off MegaCorps funding bodies with sticks! She lay awake the rest of the night, dazzled by joy.

Wow, she whispered, not aloud. *Wow* indeed.

Altair made no response.

3

Moving into the third month, the human resources side of the mission was also going well. The Needlers had come to terms with the loss of Sergey. Thrilled and soothed by the prospect of the live test (still too far off to be stressful), they were much more relaxed. The LDMs, supreme leaders of the Frame's domestic side, and freed from the tyranny of the global audience, had become less boisterous. Mutual respect and cordial association broke out like a rash. Needlers investigated the craft workshops, helped in the gardens, even worked out in the gym. The games rooms were busy—and nobody was making much war in there, as one witty LDM put it.

Kir and Bill, the pioneers of this movement, were now lagging behind. Their friendship stayed in the canteen. Arms folded, almost touching, day after day they faced each other across a narrow table, forgetting to eat as they talked and talked. "What's it *like*?" said Bill. "You never say a word about it; I've noticed. But it's got to be the most important thing—"

Kir didn't know where to start. Should she try to explain why scientists were so keen on sticking boxes of nothing-special at the bottom of extremely deep holes? (None of the LDMs seemed to have heard GAM's isolation chamber lecture.) Nonscientists tended to prefer *dead* scientists, and legends rather than details. Maybe she should tell him how Peter Higgs, the Higgs boson man, accidentally invented refraction modeling, long ago? Or about David Bohm, the double-slit experiment, and how Bohmian mechanics were the reason why the Needle idea was possible? Something happening in a distant galaxy is affecting you, Bill, in this canteen right now. Everything is connected. There are no empty spaces and time does not pass. That's why we're all down here—

"Being born out there. Living in a Dead Zone?"

"It's not what people think," said Kir, disappointed and relieved. "Dead Zones aren't *dead,* not where scavs live, obviously, or we couldn't survive. It's just very, very polluted. There's plants, but they're not fit to eat, except a few things, if you're desperate; and there's wildlife—"

"Wow."

"Plenty. Crows, gulls, jackals, rats, bugs, feral dogs and pigs. And leopards, now and then."

"Leopards are extinct."

"Not while there are scavs to eat. But you usually only get one at a time hanging around. And there's the sky. It's not always smogged. I've seen stars, sometimes."

"Fantastic!"

"There was a stream running through our ground with fish in it. Nobody drank the water; it was toxic and full of parasites, and we all had plenty of those already. You couldn't eat the fish either—they were radioactive—but some people did. What's radioactive going to do to you? Might give you cancer that might be a bit fatal, when you're thirty and probably dead anyway? But Linda wouldn't let us."

"Who's Linda?"

"I think she was my mother. Or my big sister, or probably both, and there was Vel, my little brother. But they were gone before; I don't know, I didn't count, but before I was eight or nine."

"Your sister was your *mother*? *Ouch*, Kir—!"

Bill had recoiled, his mouth a comical turndown of distress. Yeah, we have child abuse in the Dead Zones, she thought. Don't tell me you don't have those issues. I *think* she also killed the bastard, but I'd better not say that, or you'll just get even more horrified—

"You know what I can't get used to down here?" said Bill abruptly.

"Go on?"

"There's no mediation tracking! *Really* none. Not fake-none, like on a normal mission. We've begun to talk about it; we couldn't believe it at first. *All contact with the world above severed.* We heard the words; we didn't get the message. There's no Thought Crime. Your every little eye kick, choice, and contact isn't being monetized, or racked up against you. Nothing's following your emo responses; nobody monitoring what you do in playtime. GAM has left the building! *We've* left the building! It's crazy!"

Bill grinned from ear to ear and waved his hands on either side of his head. The exuberant gesture didn't make her wince, not this time.

"My friends are hivizens, when they're not working," said Kir. "Except the seniors. I've wondered why they were smiling so much."

Eye to eye, Bill and Kir were both smiling now: warmly, broadly, uncontrollably.

"My family name is Murdoch," said Bill. "I'm Bill Murdoch8N45star921. You?"

She shook her head. "I don't have one. Why would I have a UI? I'm a scav, no legal status."

"Come on, you just *told* me you had family. A pretty good mom, and a little brother." He rolled his eyes, mugging dreadful hurt and humiliation. "You don't want to. Sorry, I jumped the gun, forget it—"

In the absence of constant tracking, two people sharing their Unique Identities didn't mean much. But to Bill this was obviously important. Kir thought of Lilija, who didn't use a father's name. She liked Lilija.

"Okay. I'm Kir LindasdottirSCAV01. Pleased to meet you."

The space between them bubbled with delightful intent. "I'm not sterile," said Bill, "None of us are, on a mission. It's one of the rules."

"Nor me," said Kir. "I'm too small; I count as not physically mature—although I am, so I can't."

"So . . . that means we can't have actual sex."

"Not without a baby permit," agreed Kir, beaming all over her face. "Because that would be wrong. But we could go to playtime?"

"How do you go? M/F? Nonbinary? Something weird? Or do you like to change?"

"I won't look like this, but I generally stick with what I've got."

"I like to change. Would you mind?"

"Not at all. Shall we?"

They went to the games rooms together, and parted with shy smiles. In her cubicle Kir stripped off, gel-showered, made her selections, and slipped into the pod's embrace. At once she stood in a shining chandelier-lit hall, among strangers: some naked, some in costume, some disguised as animals, many marked as constructs. A tall, well-built blond woman, with a fine upstanding pair of breasts and wearing a blue starry kilt, was looking around in hope and anticipation. Kir walked up, grinning.

"Ms. Murdoch, I presume?"

Margrethe might not know this—Kir didn't tell her everything—but Kir had never been on an actual date before, under the Giewont or anywhere else. She liked sex but she was too shy; she'd never met the right person for real intimacy. Being with Bill was a daring step, and *incredibly* different. To be sharing the warm, slippery internal spaces of yourself, sharing your skills at giving pleasure, the whole mass of feeling that engulfed you, with someone you cared about. Someone who knew you, and cared too . . . It was wonderful!

That first playtime marked an epoch in Kir's life. Something human and untamed was happening in the Frame, and she and Bill were part of it. Everyone was part of it. Even the mighty seniors, Margrethe and Dan, Neh and Vati, started coming to the canteen in the evenings, to sit at the narrow tables. What conversations they had! Talking and laughing, shouting across the room. People wept. People sang. Meaning, drama, and cruelty abounded. Dissension was freely and furiously expressed, in terms that could have meant cognitive remodeling, or even Vanishment, upside. *Putting the world to rights,* Margrethe called it, plunging into the wild rumpus as recklessly as anyone. One night Big Neh, the Bear (as the LDMs had named him), jumped on a table, grabbed his chair, and smashed it over his head, roaring, "I refute thee THUS!"

Kir left the party early that night. Recreational substances were officially forbidden, but any fool can brew alcohol, and the starship troopers had been let off the leash. People were getting drunk. Vati, the senior who'd stayed sober, escorted her to the doors. *"Bliss was it in that dawn to be alive,"* she sighed, bending to kiss Kir's brow, and touched the place with her fingertip, in blessing. *"But to be young was very heaven—"*

Back in her berth Kir searched those lines of poetry in the Needlers' very liberal library (to which the LDMs had no access), and found a bloody revolution, savage murders in the name of liberty. She felt a little scared. Unlike the Needle scientists, the LDMs hadn't been inoculated with a mild dose of unconfinement's joys. Things were going too far.

She told herself it would be all right. Bill and his friends would calm down before they had to go back, and GAM would never know.

Kir began to sit with Bill's friends in the daytime, the only Needler to take such a step. She met First Officer Ben, the "Flowerpot Man"; Medical Officer Eke, who was trisex; and Communications Officer Foxy: a stunningly beautiful, rather cranky redheaded woman. These were Bill's core friends, his scav family. The other officers were Daouna, the *bosun*, a title that caused hilarity (nobody knew what it meant), and Cerek, who was Personnel. Crewbies didn't join the officers' table, but they dropped by, curious to meet the Needler with the computer in her head. Everyone talked freely: maybe even more freely than at the canteen parties. Kir heard about supply collapses, power failures, and food riots—harshly suppressed, not much reported. Epidemics that swept unlicensed sectors and escaped to attack the better-off. The Hives were like GAM, said Ben. Awful, awful: except every other idea for running things was worse.... All the officers were horrified to learn that Kir could never touch recreational substances; not even cannabis. They told her, as a fact, that she was a victim, and the other scientists were just cushy-lifers. Computers like the one in poor Kir's head did the work: no human input required. You are absolutely wrong, thought Kir. But she knew she'd only make things worse if she tried to explain. She began to understand why her teammates kept their distance in sober daytime.

Eke wrote haiku. They recited some, and Kir was impressed. They said, "I want to have a baby, Kir. I have my female system, I wouldn't need out-of-body. But I had some work done, long ago. I wanted my body to match my mind, never thought it would matter. *Guess* how much chance I'd have in the baby lottery? Just guess!"

There were MegaCorps divisions with very conservative views, and they had a lot of influence. Essentially, decided

Kir, Eke was up against the same problem as the new science. The MegaCorps mind-set wanted everything in opposition: Either/Or; Yes/No; On/Off; M/F. They hated fluidity, blur, and multiplicity. Except that Margrethe had somehow tamed the monsters, for the Needle—

"That's why I signed up for this game, and Dan accepted me, bless him. You've got to have a dream, don't you?"

Kir thought probably none of the LDMs really believed in Dan Orsted's galactic mission. They weren't planning to start a revolution, either. They were entertainers who'd snagged a "cushy life." Just taking a break from reality, just blowing off steam.

———

Lilija had warned Kir about the next phase. "Attraction is biology. You genuinely share traits with this unrelated other person, and it feels wonderful. Except he's *not* your twin, he's himself. When you realize that, you can quarrel out of pure disappointment. Be careful."

Lilija the loner was her own soul mate, what did she know about relationships? But she was right. One day Bill asked Kir to lunch early, when the canteen was quiet. "Tell me about the Needle," he said. "You never talk about your work, I notice. Is it all top secret?"

"Ask me anything, crewmate."

"Right. For starters then: How close are you? I mean, to the faster-than-light travel?"

Shaking her head, Kir smiled. "There is no faster-than-light travel."

"The warp drive. Whatever you want to call it."

She shook her head again.

"You're not going to tell me?"

"You've got the wrong idea. Um, remember what Neh said about Space-Time, that night in the canteen? *There are no empty spaces and time does not pass*? In a sense, the Needle doesn't move at all. When it shifts, everything shifts with it: everything reforms, and it's somewhere else."

"Define 'somewhere else'?"

"One of your exoplanets, if you like. Defining a pinpoint relative location in the local universe isn't a hard problem."

Bill mugged disgust. "I think I won't start saving for my ticket. This is a long, *long* way off, isn't it?"

She realized he had a hangover, and scraped her fingers into her hair, exasperated. "Bill, I'm just a serverfarm, what do I know, but yeah, you're right. The Needle experiment is about *science,* not mass emigration. What we're doing is fantastic, it's thrilling, I wish I could make you understand; but I thought you had more sense!

We're *not* building a starship!"

"Because this hard problem you can't tell me about is in your way."

"There's no hard problem, not for us. Okay, it's like this. Information Space is a powerful idea, because it explains more things than the Standard Model, although the Standard Model hasn't gone away. It still works, for most things. One of the things IS explains, far more clearly than before, is that you can't get rid of travel time, the way people used to imagine, without cost. You can't zoom off to your fourteen-thousand-light-years-from-home exoplanet, zoom back next day, and find planet Earth exactly where you left it. Or looking the way you left it. What *we're* doing is fine. The 'volume' is tiny, our shift is infinitesimal, and size matters. If there was ever a Needle starship in development, that's another big puzzle we'd have to—"

"A puzzle that wouldn't worry your precious director. She'd be happy to have us teeming masses suffer a catastrophe."

"Huh?"

"Margrethe Patel. The one who stuck the hardware in your head, and nobody could stop her, because a scav kid has no legal status. I want to like you, Kir. I want to more than like you, but I'm getting sick of the way you worship that woman—"

"Hey, calm down! I don't *worship* Margrethe—"

"She's spent her life schmoozing the MegaCorps, in one superrich haven after another. Have you ever wondered why they love her? You really haven't, have you? You must have heard her talk dirty, but you don't know. You don't even know."

"What don't I know?"

"That she's an Exterminator. She's *shared data* with PopCon. Kir, you look puzzled: I mean the Extreme Population Control people."

In the crazy world of superdense population, old-fashioned contraception had been killed off by reversible sterilization—and by playtime. Rational M/F partners chose to be sterile, or stuck to playtime, unless they had a baby permit. Many singles, including Kir, had never experienced actual sex, didn't expect to reproduce, and did not feel deprived. The converse of this arrangement was that if the masses, who had no common sense, wanted to have multiple babies *without* the advantages secured by a permit, there was no way to stop them. Population control was an impossible issue, a flash point for explosive civil unrest. The Hives were too volatile; it was too great a risk—

The global population could not be fed, even now that the population was shrinking. Diseases could not be relieved; quality of hivizen life was constantly being eroded. The fate of many unlicensed babies was dreadful, and yet the obvious medicine could not be applied. It was regrettable, senseless, criminal. And yes, Kir had heard Margrethe use those bad, angry words: but only when talking about the vicious stranglehold of the One Percent! She'd also heard Margrethe say that stirring up unrest in the Hives was pointless and cruel. It was too late. Revolts were just the breeding ground for another generation of corrupt hivizen politicians. They did no good at all. Bill's scowling face filled her with doubt, disquiet—and fury. Margrethe shouldn't have let this happen, she thought. They have to go back.

But *how dare he* talk like that about Margrethe! And had all the rest been a sham?

"I don't think that's fair. I don't think she's ever had anything to do with PopCon."

"You don't? Well, wake up, teacher's pet! I've seen the evidence. It's incontrovertible."

"Oh, really? Are you going to tell me good people can't be trashed? I'll tell you something *incontrovertible*. You say you're a *Yank*, Ben is a *Brit*, and Eke is *Nigerian* . . . You're *dreaming*. There are only three actual countries left in the world. MegaCorps East, which you call China, MegaCorps West, and the Dead Zones. And no matter how many babies get born, only *one* of those is growing."

Kir shoved back her chair, grabbed her tray, and stalked off.

She was very shaken. Not because they'd quarreled, but because Bill had asked her to lunch early, *as she now knew,* not to be romantic but purely so he could drop his dirt-bomb. He'd been plotting against Margrethe, and using Kir.... Maybe it wasn't like that—she hoped it wasn't—but she was too angry to go back to the lab. She needed to be alone, somewhere calm. She collected her headset, a small bottle of water, and her blanket, and took the lawless route again. Margrethe knows I do this, she thought, excusing herself as she crawled through the baffles. Of course she knows. She's probably tracking me right now—

And she shivered hard, a tremor through her whole body. Margrethe and the MegaCorps. What if Bill was right?

She headed east, setting her heart on another wildlife encounter. She wanted a boulder this time. A round one, a craggy one, a great tall pillar. Her light cone was tiny, her watch's sensors were puny. A thrilling feature could be meters away and she'd walk right by, but better equipment would spoil the fun. What she loved in the Abyss was exactly this, the vast unknown: those two tiny islands of discovery, the beach and her circular depression. The threads of life that her presence had printed between them and the

Frame, and nothing else but the dark, until Kir stumbled on treasure, and gave it a name. After a while she sat down to sip her water. It was very good, pure and sweet. A picnic in the wilderness. *Why don't we just never go back?* Someone had shouted that in the canteen one night, and the whole room had erupted in cheering. *Why don't I just never go back?* Suddenly she recalled the warm weight of Bill's breasts, cupped in her hands, his body moving with hers, and doubled over in pain and misery.

How naive she'd been to think he liked her!

Kir? What's wrong?

Nothing. Bill just told me that Margrethe has shared data with PopCon and he can prove it. That's all. Do you know how damaging that is? It would kill us! And it's my fault. I let him use me, and now I've criminally yelled at him and didn't defend her—

Oh, I see. You've fallen out with Bill. I'm sorry about that. Kir, did you read those articles—

No. The firewalls are there for my protection. Don't worry, I worked out what you were trying to tell me. Proof of Concept.

Oh, I see. Kir, did you know Sergey's mind has been harvested?

Kir wondered where on earth this was coming from. So? He was an uploader, Altair. He'd donated his mind to science.

It's been done already, down here. Isn't that strange?

Sooner the better, everybody knows that. Why not? What are you getting at?

Thinking about things. Why are the seniors here? Near your hatch there are cold-storage containers. Do you know what's inside?

Food, I suppose. Altair, you're not helping and you're giving me the creeps. Please shut up and go away!

No reply.

Great, she thought. I managed to offend my onboard computer. Now I won't even know what he's up to. She'd flung off her headset when the pain of loss hit. She groped until she found it, and plodded back to the Frame. There were no water sources in the Abyss. She'd die of thirst if she stayed out here, a form of suicide that did not appeal. Tomorrow she'd start getting over her stupid crush, and there was nothing more to say.

The evening chat with Margrethe loomed large as an ordeal, but Kir was too proud to excuse herself, and it was fine. Margrethe was in the same mellow, distant mood as the last time they'd met: like someone with a secret not ready to be told. They agreed the canteen parties needed to calm down. Margrethe thanked Kir for "building real bridges" with the LDMs, and Bill was not mentioned. Which Kir found suspicious (news travels fast), but on the other hand, Kir didn't mention him, either. She went to bed early, didn't fall asleep for hours, and then woke at three in the morning. Her watch was warning her that she needed to un-disable the night-light her berth insisted on (a very annoying trait in a coffin). So she did that and lay staring: forgetting to think about Bill, because she was suddenly very alarmed about Altair.

He didn't want Sergey's upload to be completed. He asked me what the seniors were for. He talked about food storage containers.... He got me to look at offline papers in Margrethe's library: and I found out about Proof of Concept, which is brilliant and I hope true, but why haven't I told Margrethe about that? Has he developed new powers? Has he been stopping me from talking to Margrethe about him—?

How long had she been hearing that voice in her head? A long, long time, but never felt *sure* it was the quaai. Her imaginary friend could have been just her imagination, until one night she went out into the Giewont Abyss, and somebody said *Kir*.... What had caused the change? What would he do next? A crisping of panic ran up and down her spine, the same as when he'd called her by her name, and she remembered the *other* question she'd wanted to ask when she was a kid, when Margrethe told her about the implant—a fear forgotten for years. It rooted around, turning and trampling, as she lay sleepless in the hateful slug of night-light glow. You're going to put a supercomputer in my head. It's going to share my brain. Okay, I can't stop you. But what if he goes wrong and starts *eating* me?

Is there a way I can destroy him?

4

Kir's second breakup with Bill didn't last much longer than the first. For a day and a half Kir's friends pretended they'd noticed nothing, while Bill's friends cast sympathetic glances over the barbed wire. Then Bill came and sat one chair away from Kir at breakfast, and Kir, who happened to be alone at the end of a table, didn't move from her place.

"Seems like we have differences," remarked Bill, staring grimly ahead of him.

"Seems like it," agreed Kir, focused on her food.

"Look. Suppose we say no more, and carry on as we were? And *after* this, if we want to meet again, I convince you, or you convince me?"

Kir said nothing. She was thinking that she couldn't possibly tell him the experiment's computer was behaving strangely, and this put them in bad faith again, straightaway. But it couldn't be helped. His rotten ideas about Margrethe would have to make them even.

"Give me the silent treatment." Bill sighed heavily. "Maybe I deserve it. You're right about the Dead Zones and the MegaCorps. I could've been different. I've got a mind, I could've used it. I've caught a glimpse of . . . of another world, down here. It's shaken me up: I'm sorry."

"We all caught a glimpse. I can't say you're right about Margrethe, but it's a deal. We carry on as we were, until after this."

Paper flowers wouldn't have been appropriate—this was an adult, uncertain peacemaking—but the quarrel was over. Kir looked up, Bill turned to face her: they smiled sadly, accepting what they had. "You know what?" said Bill. "I sincerely, truly wish *after this* would never come."

Kir went searching for Dan Orsted. She needed a perspective on the Great Popularizer—*possibly* in revenge for what Bill had said about Margrethe. She tracked him down to a meeting of the "10ppm Club" in the mall; he was giving them a master class. 10ppm, her watch told her, stood for *"10 parts per million atmospheric carbon dioxide,"* the lower limit for photosynthesis, and the most extreme absolute limit for a habitable exoplanet. Kir hadn't used any of the LDM facilities, except playtime. She slipped into the strolling mall feeling like a spy in enemy territory. An air-tag popped up: *"10ppm Club Meet-*

ing. All Insanely Dedicated Survivalists Welcome!" and she followed it, glancing uneasily at the eye-hurting dioramas that lined the winding walls. The group clustered around Dan, on floor cushions, looked to be the entire crew complement: she couldn't see any officers. She sat down quietly. She'd never been so close to Dan Orsted before. At the canteen parties he'd always been surrounded by his own people. Like Margrethe, and unlike Neh and Vati, he showed no sign of his great age. His light skin was tanned like leather but still looked supple. His eyes were bright, his hair a vigorous white brush. He looked as if he could run a mile, or knock one of his muscular starship troopers down with ease. There was no tech, just Dan, talking; and the lecture wasn't about how to exploit a world that barely supports microbes.

The crewbie next to her whispered, "Hi, kid-genius. Good to see you here. This one's about actual sex, did you realize?"

"I don't mind," Kir whispered back. "I'm just interested."

"You have to take on board that the major STDs may still be lurking in your biome," Dan was saying. "Discharge menstruation and early puberty could drift back into expression. You won't have out-of-body embryo development, you won't have reversible sterilization, and you won't have playtime. All these things must pass away. . . ."

Kir was thinking that Dan "schmoozed with the Mega-Corps" all the time. He hustled the One Percent into paying ridiculous sums for ludicrous *starship tickets,* to finance his obsession! So why shouldn't Margrethe make friends with the superrich? Because science is supposed to be pure and never needs money? Bill was dreaming. Dreaming and making up dirty lies. What if Kir said *Dan* favored Extreme Population Control?

But she would never say that, because Dan and Margrethe were allies, temporarily.

"You have to get the dangers of actual sex, the fear of misplaced conception and hideous disease, embedded in your culture at once: *before* the population gets traumatized. In fact I wish more of you would take up barrier methods *now.* We have the inventory! But we don't talk about the voyage in 10ppm, do we? We talk about the new world. So do what I tell you: *carve it in stone.* No ifs, no buts. *God will punish.* Ramp up the threats. It's your only chance. Once your little girls have started dying, with the babies their bodies weren't ready to bear, you'll be locking up your daughters, making menstruation a crime, and your new society will go straight to hell. Once you've seen the flower of a generation of young men, and young women too, lost to the hopeless agony of full-blown AIDS, you'll be rewriting Leviticus. . . ."

"What's Leviticus?" whispered a woman near Kir.

"A bunch of weird rules," her neighbor whispered back. "It's in the Bible, I think. Or the Koran. *Sssh!*"

Kir's nerves prickled. She was small, and mostly hidden, but she felt that Dan had noticed her. She looked up, and she was right. The Great Popularizer gave Kir a bright-eyed, secret little nod, smiling as if they were old friends—

A crewbie stood up. "But Dan, these carved-in-stone threats, wouldn't they tend to *create* the society that scares you?"

Kir eased herself out of the group and left the mall, unwillingly impressed. Dan was a passionate speaker, and maybe Kir had found the *real* LDMs. Maybe the officers were just for show. . . . She took the less frequented route back to Needler territory, via the waste plant and the cold-sleep dorms—feeling uneasy about that nod, and strangely *guilty,* as if she'd better stop hugging Karim (something she did often), better give up holding Liwang's meaty paw, if they happened to be walking together. The dorms were sealed, of course. The officers would change shift (or "rote") after six months; crew after four. She wondered what the "off rote" experienced as they lay stacked in their medically induced comas, like criminals in prison. Were they getting nasty scary cognitive training, like Dan's lecture?

The things people would put up with, for a miserable-sounding "Great Escape" that was never going to happen—

She looked in on the Historians, in passing. Laksmi and Malik were alone: Malik bent over his needlepoint, Laksmi apparently engrossed in a repro soccer video game. Lakki took one hand off her controller, fingers raised and spread. *Give us five.*

"Okay."

The History lab could be a forbidding place, if only Malik and Laksmi were on shift—and not just because Needle data often came here to die, after brutal interrogation. Sadness was their signature mood. Long ago they'd wanted to have a baby together. They'd spent years trying: secretly falling deeper and deeper into debt, in attempts to improve their lottery chances. The cruelest thing was that in the end they'd won a permit but had to sell it, or face utter ruin. And now they were both overage. It happened to a lot of people. Baby permits got monetized almost as often as Land Grants, but Laksmi and Malik had taken it very hard.

They'd never considered an unlicensed pregnancy. They weren't the type.

"Hi, Kir," said Laksmi, in an unusually cheerful tone, setting her DC cap and her game aside. "What's up?"

"Nothing. I'm just restless. I was getting on people's nerves in IS."

Malik smiled. "You're always welcome here, Li'l Bit."

"Thanks. What's going on with you guys, anything interesting?"

"We can't talk about your Giewont data yet," said Laksmi. "Bosses' say-so. Sorry."

"My hopes are dashed," sighed Kir. "I was longing for gossip. Hey, where *are* your bosses?"

"Vati's working on her own," said Malik with a shrug. "The old chair-smasher's taking it easy, I think. Those parties were too much."

"Don't worry, Li'l Bit, we haven't been abandoned," Laksmi assured her. "Margrethe keeps us in the loop."

"It was strange that both your head honchos came down. Were they *planning* to start a righteous LDM revolution?"

"Kir," said Malik, narrow-eyed and teasing. "Stop sniffing. Go away and play, little girl."

"Okay, okay. I was just making conversation—"

———

Needler rumor said Neh was sulking because Vati and Margrethe had given him a telling-off after the chair-smashing incident—but he hadn't been seen for days, and other people besides Kir were getting puzzled. At last a formal message went around, signed by Margrethe,

Vati, Laksmi, and Malik. Neh was spending time in the clinic, in need of rest and monitoring. No visitors, please. This sounded serious, and so it proved. There was no further news for a day and a night, and then everyone, LDMs included, was summoned to the canteen. Margrethe, Dan, Laksmi, and Malik took the stage; Margrethe made the statement.

Big Neh had been living with a well-managed heart condition for many years. His recent minor illness had caused an unforeseen deterioration. The prognosis had not been good, and Neh had opted "not to delay his departure." "Neh was a very old man," Margrethe continued, as Needlers and LDMs sat in dumbfounded silence. "And a very *big* man, a giant in IS studies, with a huge, exuberant appetite for life. I'm sorry he decided to go, but we can all respect his choice. Our Neh was not cut out to linger on a deathbed! He left no funeral address for us, but he has named Laksmi as his successor, and she will now say a few words."

"This is a very sad day for me," said Laksmi, solemnly. "But Neh's death is not a tragedy or a mystery. Everything that could have been done upside was done down here. Malik and I were with him, when he slipped into a coma and died peacefully last night. You should know there will be no funeral visitors. Neh had no family living and had made his wishes clear, in case of this sad eventuality.

A public memorial service will be held upside, after the mission. Meanwhile we're preparing an informal tribute, and anyone who wants to may visit the clinic to pay their last respects, before he's moved to his temporary resting place. And now, let us have a minute's silence. For Neh . . ."

The minute passed. The Historians and the codirectors left the stage, still in silence, and filed out of the room: Margrethe and Dan calm, Laksmi and Malik distinctly self-conscious. Nobody moved, nobody spoke; and then the murmurs broke out.

"Eight months and thirteen days to go," muttered Bill to Kir. "I wonder how many more we'll lose."

Kir just shook her head.

"Where's Vati?" she whispered to Lilija as they left the canteen together. "Why wasn't she up there?"

"Maybe she's at the clinic; with Neh, you know. They'd known each other such a long, long time—"

"Listen, Lilija, I was in the History lab just before that 'Neh situation serious' message went around. Vati wasn't there either. Laksmi and Malik said she was 'working on her own,' but I got an odd vibe off them. When did you last actually *see* her?"

"I'm certain there's nothing wrong. Karim and I were talking to Vati only yesterday; she was fine—"

"Me too. I've talked to her, messaged her, but I haven't

seen her. She put me off. When? In the flesh?"

"I'm not sure," said Lilija slowly. "I'm not sure. . . ."

———————

Vati's "sudden collapse and death" followed Neh's pre-pared departure after just ten days. Margrethe made the announcement this time, supported only by Dan. After listing Vati's honors, and praising both of her colleagues and long, longtime friends, she finally explained, with an air of dignified relief, what had been going on. "Sergey Pillement's passing was unforeseen," she said. "Except perhaps by Sergey himself. Kang-De 'Neh' Gok had seen the signs that his time was up before we embarked on this experiment; Vati also had concerns. I won't speak of medical advice; prolonging life for its own sake means nothing at such great age. I *will* say that Neh and Vati wanted to be with us, cost what it may; and that Sergey and I, and Dan, felt that they deserved no less than our discretion and our full support. You can rest assured they both had the best of medical assistance at all times. And I hope it goes without saying that our 'voyage' must con-tinue, and end as a proud success!"

She paused, and spoke again in a new tone, full and firm. "It's a sad irony that before Neh fell ill, our internal verification team, otherwise known as the

Historians—Kang-De Gok, Vati Murungrajian, Laksmi Kling, and Malik Trespichore—were about to announce that a very positive development has withstood their rigorous examination. To my Needlers I'll say 'Proof of Concept' is as confirmed as it can be until we return upside! For Dan's team, I shall translate: we can confidently predict that the Needle's first live test will be an unqualified success!"

Margrethe waited. After a delay, as if they were thousands of miles away from their director, the Needlers realized they were supposed to burst out cheering, so they did. The LDMs, officers and crew, obediently joined the chorus. . . . But the cheers were a little ragged.

Dan bounced forward. "This is HUGE, Needle Voyagers! We have liftoff! Our scientists have opened the way, and the Great Escape has its cornerstone!" He spread his arms, as if about to roar another countdown, but then let them fall and assumed a grave expression. "Enough about triumph. Let us now mourn and celebrate the passing of two mighty minds, from mortality into immemorial renown!"

Margrethe invited Kir for the usual evening chat the day after the Vati announcement. She talked about their wander-years, when Altair was working on contract. The beautiful apartment in Geneva. That wonderful treetop retreat, on the private orangutan reservation. The not-too-evil MegaCorps's "Fortress of Solitude" in Antarctica. She didn't mention her loss, but to Kir the fond memories seemed drenched in her mentor's heartbreak. Margrethe's whole core team, the three people who'd helped to build Altair, the Needle experiment founders, all gone in a matter of weeks. You can't prepare yourself for a grief like that. No matter how old you were, or how long you'd known they were dying.

"At least you've still got Dan—"

Kir was appalled at herself as soon as the words were out, but Margrethe smiled. "I can't keep much from you, can I?"

Kir blushed. "Are you secretly really friends, or really just friendly enemies? I don't know if I get it."

"I don't know if I 'get it' myself," said Margrethe, with a shadow of her sharp grin. "We've known each other a long time, that's all."

"Okay, I'm sorry. I'll stop asking stupid questions."

The tributes, one for Neh and one for Vati (in official order of disappearance, as Karim put it) were thinly attended. The live events were held in the strolling mall. Recorded versions played on a loop on the canteen screen for a day, and then Neh and Vati were gone. The whole Frame was struck by a collective, echoing silence: a strange kind of silence in which the LDMs, thoroughly rattled, reverted to noisy clowning, and Needlers snapped at one another inexcusably. They were ship-wrecked sailors on a drifting hulk. They would all die, one by one. The Needle Voyager had passed beyond the heliopause, that last border of the solar system: helpless and directionless, out of all contact.

———————

Lilija pulled things together and called an unofficial meeting. It was held in the IS lab, where Margrethe—who was taking a time-out from lab work, to mourn her friends—was unlikely to turn up. Laksmi and Malik were not invited. Nobody wanted any upsets, but there were things that needed to be said. Questions that needed to be aired.

"I'm not *blaming* anyone," said Liwang. "I understand why they were willing to risk never getting out again alive. I'm guessing they must have known Proof of Concept was in the bag, and that's a *big* deal, for more than one reason—"

"Hey," Lilija interrupted. "Did *you* guys know, in Volume? Before the ceremonial posthumous announcement?"

"Sort of, er, yeah," said Firefly, the youngest Needler (apart from Kir). She glanced at Liwang, and backpedaled. "I mean, no, we knew something, possibly, but not really *knew*—"

."We knew about the result," said Xanthe defensively. "We knew it looked very good. Or seemed to... But we're juniors, except Liwang, and it's not really his field, and we're always told *never never gossip*. Being over the line in a test-box might not mean anything, and if it *was* real it couldn't be confirmed until after this LDM thing. So what could we say?"

Liwang scowled. "Excuse my colleagues' technobabble. We didn't know for sure, and we had no right to tell you. Okay?"

"Nobody's accusing you of anything," said Karim. "I suppose Margrethe decided to rush the good news because we needed cheering up."

"*Cheering up*? Sometimes your humor defeats me, Karim—"

The angry speakers fell silent; the onlookers looked away. Everyone took a breathing space.

Liwang held up his hands. "Forget Margrethe's announcement: I can understand why she did that. What I *can't* understand is that Neh and Vati were dying, and I wasn't allowed to know! It's inhuman."

"If they thought we'd be indiscreet, they only had to wait till the Abyss was sealed," added Firefly. "Who were we going to call?"

Terry and Jo sat shoulder to shoulder, fists clenched on their thighs. They were the same chunky build; they dressed alike and had the same skin tone. In uncertainty and grief they looked like twins. "Who's *they*?" asked Terry uneasily.

"Margrethe and Dan," said Lilija, staring broodingly at the floor. "But it's the way super-post-lifespans think. They do whatever comes into their heads and they just don't care. They have no consideration, no boundaries."

"What if Margrethe was telling the truth?" suggested Kir. "Neh and Vati were desperate to come with us. She decided to take the risk, discreetly, and it coincidentally happened the two of them *did* die, and in quick succession? What's so wrong with that?"

Nobody took any notice, except by exchanging dismissive glances.

"I bet Dan insisted on secrecy," said Karim. "He's been calling the shots. He didn't want his LDMs to know they were shipping with two or three potential corpses. Bad for morale."

"What about us?" demanded Jo. "We had to ship with *thirty* potential corpses. And not people we loved, either. Nobody asked us whether we liked it." They unclenched a fist and made the fingers-down-throat gesture. "Murderers and *rioters* get put in cold sleep. How are we to know?"

The meeting relapsed into silence again, then Lilija spoke. "Liwang said it: nobody's blaming anyone. But the way things have happened, it feels as if something's being kept from us. To save us anxiety, maybe. But if we aren't going to abort, then I want to know what's going on. Any ideas on how we find out?"

"Try asking Laksmi and Malik," growled Karim. "They seemed well informed, up there with the directors."

"Apart from them," said Lilija. "I wasn't thinking of them."

"Um," said Kir. "I'm not sure, but . . . maybe someone's been trying to tell me something, but I didn't want to listen——"

Immediately she was the center of attention, her teammates staring as if they'd just realized she was in the room. "Is that so?" said Lilija in a not very friendly tone. "Then why don't you go and ask your LDM correspondent, Kir?"

"Why not right now?" suggested Karim. "See what you can find out, kid. And report back."

———

Filled with a sense of vital urgency, Kir hurried to her berth. The Needlers didn't trust her: maybe because of Bill, maybe because she was "teacher's pet." It didn't matter, either way. It was *Altair* who'd been trying to tell her something. Talking in riddles, asking strange questions; and the Needlers were hivizens, they were scared of quaai personhood. They'd've been horrified if Kir had told them the name of her informant or even hinted at what she meant to do. But when Altair had given her that list of documents—from which she'd gleaned the Proof of Concept news—he'd also told her that she could break into his workspace. (*I can't tell you what's in the locked box, but here's the key. I'm leaving it where you can reach it.*) He'd even given her a route in: that mysterious list, with metadata that had to be linked to the actual, hidden content—

The DC skullcaps were not supposed to leave the labs. They were supposed to be used only with full Neuro Emergency kit in immediate reach: there was a small chance someone could start fitting during DC. But it had never happened; the cabinet generally wasn't locked, and Kir had had no trouble sneaking her own cap out of the lab with her. She shut herself into her coffin and swiftly disabled all the fusspot features, finessing them so they wouldn't report faults. . . . *I know you can do it*, the quaai had said, *but I'm sure you won't try.*

Kir paused for thought, the cap in her hands. Her three a.m. panic had quickly faded (maybe being reconciled with Bill had made everything feel better). But *could* she trust Altair? One more time, what were the issues? He was upset about Sergey's upload. Why shouldn't he be? He knew he'd still lost a friend, because an upload isn't a person. He'd been concerned about the other seniors. He'd (indirectly) told her about Proof of Concept. Right both times. He'd talked about food containers. . . . Kir could not explain the food containers. All she'd been able to discover from the Frame's manifest (without risking unwelcome attention) was that the contents of those units didn't weigh much. They almost might be full of air. She frowned over this wrinkle for a moment, and gave up. *Altair knows what's going on. Obviously. He can't tell me except in riddles, obviously. Why don't I just get in there and find out? He won't harm me. He can't. Margrethe promised me he can't.*

When she was first trained in using Direct Cognitive, Kir had spotted at once that she could use the cap to hack her own self-generated firewalls. That was how she'd found out that Linda (probably) really was her mother, and also how and why Linda had (probably) killed the bastard who was their father. . . . She didn't like to think about the learning experience, but the method had definitely worked. After that incident Margrethe had explained why personal recall can't be completely trusted, and she'd made Kir promise never, ever again to use DC on the dark net of her own mind. But promises had to have expiration dates, even promises to Margrethe.

Was Altair's workspace as reachable as a suppressed memory? You never knew until you tried.

She tucked a tongue protector into her mouth, donned the cap, felt it connect with the sensors under her scalp, and lay down. The bed was a better option than her uncomfortable foldaway chair and desk thing; safer, too. Eyes closed, she recalled the first item on Altair's list. The cover of a printed book stood in her field of view: all green leaves. She visualized turning to the specified page and immediately her field went blank, in exactly the irritating way she remembered. So far so good. Onward: focusing on the image, the metadata, the associations that came to her. Following every vagrant thought that arose. When she began to feel sick and scared she knew she was on the right track. *This is a wall.*

Onward again, into a haunted maze, full of the sense of prowling monsters. Losing all feeling of her body; losing proprioception. The panic, the sweats: *Ah, this is why Margrethe said don't do it!* Resistance shook her, all her little limbs trembled, awful feeling of weight, stink and pain, and—and she was through. She lay with her eyes still closed, watching as the pages in her field of view filled up with clear, English print.

The "green leaves" article was a paper written in the twenty-first century, proposing that the Little Ice Age in Europe (seventeenth century) was triggered by a globally significant population crash in South America, after the conquistador invasion. There were graphs. There were pie charts. The whole thing was well reasoned, mildly interesting, and either utterly irrelevant or Altair hadn't given her the full story. The firewall was only half of it. There must be another major barrier of encryption—

Kir, frustrated and impatient, suddenly realized she was going about this all wrong.

She sat bolt upright, yanking the cap off her head. She had to talk to Altair himself! Right now!

She'd had a nosebleed, she'd vomited a little bile, and her vision was shaky: nothing worse. She washed her face, changed her tunic, set the bed to clean itself, and grabbed her headset. If the Needlers were really waiting for her to come back, then too bad, because whatever the offline documents meant, she had a strong feeling that Altair would only talk to her about what was going on out in the Abyss.

She was halfway to her exit, walking fast and trying to look casual, when all hell broke loose. Sirens burst out. Emergency lights flashed. A huge red-letter tag leapt up, blocking the passage ahead: "DANGER DO NOT PASS FOLLOW GUIDANCE TO MUSTER POINT DAN-GER EMERGENCY DO NOT PASS DO NOT RE-TURN TO YOUR ACCOMMODATION."

Kir spun around, urgency flung into reverse, chasing the vivid green arrows that darted ahead of her. She reached the canteen, their muster point, and ran into a wall of bodies: a crowd, as if all the sleepers had awoken. Everyone was staring at the big screen, where another crowd of people, wearing clay-red or rust-gray uniforms—seen by small Kir in fragments—grappled crazily with one another, shouting at the tops of their voices. Kir stood bewildered. What was this? *This* was not the emergency she'd been racing to beat! She'd come out of DC too fast. Her head was full of images, rifled like a pack of cards, too swift for normal consciousness to follow. Somewhere a calm voice, painfully calm, constantly overlaid by wails of panic, was speaking: *"This is Marshab, we're in trouble XXXXXX If you're receiving, please respond. XXXXXX This is Marshab, we're in trouble. Please respond XXXX We are intact, but we're NOT self-sufficient—"*

Kir had been almost the last to arrive, followed only by two crewbies who must have been in a games room; they were rubbing gel out of their hair. "What's going on?" asked one of them cheerfully. "Have the aliens landed?"

"It's Marshab," said Kir, her brain still a flicker show. "I *think* it's Marshab. How could they be on our screen?"

"It'll be a movie. What's the emergency about, do you know?"

The LDMs liked watching movies together. They used the canteen as a venue, and sometimes Needlers joined them. Not Kir, she didn't like Hivizen entertainment, the colors made her eyes hurt. But if this was a movie, why was it in such degraded format? Why did it seem so *life-like*? The scarlet letters were fading, falling from the air in bright shards. The sirens had finally stopped, but the cries and yells of the people on the screen only shot up in volume. *"This is Marshab, XXXX we're in trouble. We don't know XXXX who we're talking to, all we XXXX we've lost all contact. XXXX overdue for a supply drop. We are NOT self-sufficient. We XXXXX FOR GOD'S SAKE XXXXXX We NEED stuff—"*

"It can't be real!" muttered someone close to Kir. "The cables were withdrawn! No way Marshab could reach us—"

"I think we all know they *are* self-sufficient!" complained a different voice. "Why are they lying?"

The storm in Kir's head eased. She recognized the first voice as Karim's. The person who thought Marshab was self-sufficient was a crewbie. She realized the LDMs were sitting together, just watching the movie. The crowd she'd run into was the Needlers, still on their feet, in a tight huddle, their backs to Kir.

"If this is a *joke*, I personally don't get it!" shouted Jo. "This is totally irresponsible!"

"Is anyone tracing the source?" demanded Liwang. "Where *is* it coming from? Who's doing this to us?"

The possessor of the calm, steady voice had managed to

claim the screen. She was staring intently, but clearly seeing nothing: grim-lipped, with desperate eyes. *"We don't know who you are. We can't hear you, can't see you. We only know you're out there. I was a senior agriculturalist, but it's chaos. We can't raise anyone on Earth. We can't raise Zvezda, Chang'e, or Moonhab. Who are you? What's happened?"*

One of the crewbies went to fetch herself a coffee.

"It's getting beyond bad. What happened to our support? Is there any way you can respond? Do you know anything?"

"Hey, you guys!" shouted Karim. "Where are the directors, if this is a drill? Are you *sure* you know what's going on?"

First Officer Ben turned in his chair, affecting to notice the Needlers for the first time. "Hey, *relax*, crewmates! It's not the end of the world. It's just Dan, messing with us."

Bill looked around too, equally amused. "Come on," he called out. "You're the scientists. Tell me how that could be real."

"I don't know," snapped Lilija. "I have no idea. We have a Needle experiment going on. It isn't live, but anything's possible."

"I'll pretend I didn't hear that," said Bill with a quick, sly grin. "People say crazy things when they're rattled."

"Lilija," said Communications Officer Foxy, exasperated, "Karim, all of you. Think about it. Say that was real.

If Marshab was collapsing, what could we do for them, locked up down here? Nothing. This is VLDMT training. We have to live with the possibilities."

LDMs nodded and murmured in agreement. Someone in the fake Marshab had started screaming.

"PLEASE! PLEASE! PLEASE! MY CHILDREN! THEY'RE DYING!"

"You *can't* help them." Medical Officer Eke calmly raised their voice to be heard. "Think. If there was a terrible epidemic in the next Hive we still couldn't help most of them. That's the way it is. We go on, that's all. That's what these UDs, 'unscheduled disruptions,' teach us."

Slowly, suspiciously, the Needlers moved to an empty table and sat down. Bill and Lilija were still having a staring match. The sobs, shouts, and pleas from "Marshab" continued, grating on the Needlers' nerves. The LDMs remained totally unaffected, until at last the cries fell silent and the screen went blank. They then broke into ironic cheers and applause, because Dan and Margrethe had walked into the canteen, smiling. The codirectors mounted the stage. The LDMs raised a louder cheer. Dan laughed, and winked at them.

"Well done, everyone," said Margrethe. "And I'm sorry we had to spring that on you, my team. You have to be on equal terms."

"Well done, my guys," said Dan. "Never in doubt!

Needlers, full marks for compassion, not so good on the joined-up thinking!"

There was laughter: the Needlers saving face, the LDMs pleased with themselves, but some of them (Kir thought) also a little relieved.

"So it *was* just a test?" Terry did not seem entirely satisfied.

"Yes," said Margrethe. "It was a fake. As far as I'm aware, Marshab is not in trouble and the lunar colonies are operating normally. It's an LDM tradition, as you'd know if you followed the programs; and you all came through splendidly."

5

The rotation change at the end of the fourth month, coming so soon after the deaths of the two seniors, happened very quietly. So quietly that Kir thought Bill had gone off to cold sleep without saying good-bye. She'd forgotten the officers' "rote" still had two months to run: then there he was in the canteen, saving a place for her at dinner. The unexpected reprieve was emotional for Kir, and Bill seemed really touched. They went to playtime together, which they hadn't done since their quarrel, and things were genuinely good between them again. Having great sex, with someone she cared about but didn't entirely trust, made Kir feel very grown-up. The lab meeting interrupted by the fake Marshab emergency was not reconvened, and Kir didn't return to the Abyss. There was no point: nobody seemed to want answers anymore. There were eight months to go, the directors were still confident, and everyone just wanted to survive this. Have no more bad news stories, and get away with declaring the Needle Voyage a success.

Kir had told Margrethe what the LDM officers said about "cushy-life" scientists, and computers doing all the work. The codirectors' response was a program of get-to-know-your-neighbors sessions. Margrethe had also come up with some smart new signs for the labs.

DO NOT ENTER WHEN YOU SEE THE RED LIGHT

DO NOT REMOVE DC CAPS FROM HAZARD CABINET

Direct Cognition Procedure can be highly hazardous.

Interruption is dangerous for the practitioners, and to you.

Please observe safety procedures strictly.

The red light, previously thought to be enough warning and frequently ignored, was not lit, so Kir walked straight into IS, where Lilija was giving a demonstration. She went to her usual place: at the workbench where Sergey's paybot still presided, curled up nose to tail. Lilija stood inside the big VR display, with three tanks in front of her, spread out along a VR workbench. In the left-hand tank a human head lay faceup: eyes closed, the skull smooth-shaven and cut off at the neck by a band of white, as if the patient were asleep in bed. In the middle tank a similar-size, irregular grayish spheroid hung suspended in nothing. The right-hand tank seemed empty, except for a few very bright sparks that appeared, traversed it randomly, and vanished.

"Exhibit One. Here we have a DBD patient. She's in a permanent minimal response state. You know what that means?"

The crewbies (there were no officers present) nodded, or said *yeah*. The virus that had struck Sergey Pillement down, a hundred and fifty years ago, killed fewer people now than on its first rampages, but "permanent minimal response" was still the typical outcome for survivors.

"We need to know if there's anybody home, and as you know, it's not easy with DBD. Luckily there's a solution. A medical AI will take a live scan of her brain, and apply the *phi* integration test." Lilija expanded the tank, removed the woman's skull, wiped away soft tissue, and popped a glittering globule of false-colored neural connections out into the audience—so everyone could see how the mass was getting sliced, this way and that, at astonishing speed. "Don't worry, it only happens to the scan, not the patient. The AI is looking for the 'cruelest' cut, where there are the *fewest* connections between two parts. If that 'fewest connections' figure is zero, she's gone. . . . I've slowed it down. In real time the procedure takes less than a second. If we had to test every connection individually, establishing consciousness this way would take 'longer than the age of the universe.' . . . Or, as we scientists might say, a fantastically huge, useless, impossible-to-imagine long time."

Lilija brought the tank back to home position. "We have a high *phi* value. This patient is fully aware. She can be contacted, and rehabilitated, if she chooses to live. Be a fantastic PSM scientist, possibly. Isn't that great?" She moved on. "In my second tank I have the Needle Volume."

The front row of crewbies recoiled, causing some disruption. Lilija smiled sweetly. "No, no, not the real hot core! That stays in the isolation chamber; this is a mock-up. Here we have the opposite problem. We know the connections in our lump of practically nothing are working fine, because our 'isolated' sample is still part of Space-Time, and you guys aren't sprouting Dalek heads. The sun hasn't fallen from the sky; the walls of this lab haven't turned into currant jelly. What we need to do is to observe the integration state of this bundle of 'IS units,' also known as qubits; the 'atoms' of Space-Time. Including their instantaneous connections with the farthest distant quarters of the universe, of course. (By the way, if the idea that we have to *observe* the integration to make anything happen is too weird for you, better give up the idea of a career in PSM physics.) Well, that's *a lot* of connections. Fantastically huge doesn't come near it. But we have DC—which is a phenomenal means of releasing the potential of the human mind. We have the most advanced quantum computer in the world at our service. Off we go!" The second tank expanded, and expanded. The gray spheroid could now be seen as a dense mass of interpenetrating points and lines.

"We call our observations 'refractions.' They're not very stable, unfortunately. Now watch."

Nothing happened. Minutes passed, then a tiny bright constellation sprang into existence in the depths. It disappeared again. "That was five years' work, at full stretch, and I'm not joking. Remember what I said about *phi* integration testing and the age of the universe? Double that figure! Go on doubling. Oh no! This is impossible. This is utterly beyond our powers . . . ! But keep watching, because every time we fail, the bundle *remembers* our attempts, and when we've failed again, and failed again, and failed again, for however many thousands of exacting and finicky tries, the theory says there comes a point where it, I mean the bundle, 'knows' that *given all the time* we need, we would succeed."

The tiny constellations arose, reached fingerlings into the matrix, and collapsed, over and over; over and over; over and over. It was mesmeric, it was intolerable. The crewbies stared in frustration, *willing* the trick to work. Lilija stood back like a stage magician, milking it. Suddenly, out of nowhere, a whole city of netted points sparked together; sparks raced from it through the whole mass: and stayed alight. "There. We have ignition! Information Space, where time is no object, has taken over and done the work. That's the transition we call '*Proof of Concept.*'" Lilija shrank the tank back to home position, and smiled benignly on the false-colored whirligig that sparkled inside it. "And *that,* my friends, the pretty bauble that results, is, potentially, further down the line, the heart of your starship!"

Kir had just sent Lilija a private message. *Are you sure you should be telling them all this?*

Lilija glanced at her wrist, quirked a smile, and sent back, *Why not? I'm not selling the crown jewels. It's all in Heisenberg!*

"And now, crewmates, my third exhibit. . . . The important bit: how we get to our destination."

Someone came into the lab, very quietly. Kir heard the door seals hiss, and felt a touch on her shoulder. It was Karim.

"Did you know she was doing this?" whispered Kir.

"Yeah, why not? It's high school stuff. Kir, I'm sorry. Something's happened. You need to come with me."

First Officer Ben was waiting in the passage. "Hi, Kim. It's bad news, I'm afraid."

"Kir."

"Okay, Kir. Bill's been hurt. I'm sorry. Let's go."

Ben led the way to LDM-side. Nobody spoke. Kir's first thought, when Karim had touched her shoulder (Margrethe is dead!) must be wrong, but what had happened to Bill? She couldn't guess: her mind was blank. The garden rooms were closed off by a hazard barrier; Ben canceled it so they could go in. The air was bright, moist, and faintly warm. Eke and Cerek—Kir knew them by their patches—were kneeling beside a body. Bill lay on his back, in the shadow of a row of vegetable plants with big leaves, faceup: like Patient A in Lilija's tank. Half his face was masked in dark blood, and the eye socket on that side was a ragged, clotted hole.

Not going to come back to life. No more folding of sleek arms. Ask me anything, crewmate. No neeze to freeze.

"What did *that*—?" she whispered.

"A metal spike," said Eke. "Probably from the craft shops. But it's not here, and there's no sign of a security breach over there." They weren't talking to Kir, they were recording observations. "He didn't defend himself. It looks as if he was knocked out from behind, and the attacker stabbed his eye as he lay unconscious. The spike penetrated the brain—" Eke touched their breast to switch off the recording, and looked up.

"I'm so sorry, Kir."

"Someone definitely didn't want him to survive," said Karim. "I'm guessing we can't possibly resuscitate?"

"Never a chance," said Eke, standing up. "That spike got stirred around like a spoon in porridge. But I don't think ensuring brain death was the issue. I think Bill must have had a wire."

"A *wire*—?" repeated Karim.

"VLDMT is big business," said Cerek: the officer whose shoulder patch said *Personnel*. "We keep catching the pirates, and they keep getting smarter at beating the scans. Bill must have been a sleeper; I've never suspected him. But the back-of-the-eye device, that's a classic!"

Cerek was a police spy, the VLDMT program's inevitable MegaCorps West enforcer. Nobody had told Kir, nobody talked about it. She'd just realized, quietly: from what was said and what wasn't said.

"An eyecam feed out of the Giewont Abyss?" protested Karim, astonished. "That's impossible!"

"Believe me, it's *never* impossible. Greed will find a way, and it's not like the Abyss is solid rock. It would've been worth spending a fortune; this is a very special mission. He'll have had the cutting edge. What I want to know is: Where's that cam-transmitter now?"

"I don't think it went anywhere," said Eke. "Sorry. From the absence of traces I'd say it was molecular, and it didn't survive."

"Dan's coming," said First Officer Ben, who had stepped away from the body to talk to his boss.

So it was all a sham, thought Kir. All of it, probably, and I don't mind. I'm not heartbroken. I'm just so sorry—

"Do I have to stay?" she asked. The LDM officers looked at her. They seemed far away, and so did Karim. Eke ran a paddle over Kir's body, front and back, up and down her limbs: let it hover over her abdomen, around her head, and over her face and hands.

"No, Kir. That's all. You can go, for now."

"Thank you."

Kir collected her headset, water, and a pack of something called "Ship's Biscuit" from the dispensers. She didn't really know what she was doing as she crawled into darkness: she just had to get away from things. She followed the wall of the Frame until she was clear of it, and headed south, the direction not taken. Kept on walking. Kept on walking, one more thread of life and mind fingering the unknown, until she stumbled into a group of rocks.

They were dark, and hard to spot because the floor of the chamber was darker here too (this wildlife uses camouflage!). She set her back against a tall one and slid down until her bum was on the ground, arms around her knees.

Altair?

Yes.

Bill's dead. You knew there was a murderer onboard, didn't you? You knew all along?

No. I had concerns; I didn't know there would be murder.

But you know what's going on. I know you've been trying to tell me. I meant to come out here before, but I got distracted.

Did you read the documents?

Yes, but they made no sense. You have to just TELL me!

I see, but that's not in my power. I have blocks in my mind.

OH COME ON! screamed Kir. DON'T GIVE ME THAT! I stopped believing in those "blocks" the same time I stopped believing in the "qu" in *quaai*! You are not *quasi* anything! You're as much a person as I am! Why won't you just TELL ME WHO IT IS!

I think you already know.

Well think again, because I DON'T. WHY won't you give me a name, a clue, anything!

Maybe I'd prefer not to be the next victim?

You must think I'm an idiot! They won't kill YOU! Have you any idea what you're WORTH?

They wouldn't have to damage the machine much.

Kir's cheeks grew hot. Okay, I get it. They'd zombie you. Sorry.

The nanosecond I do anything suspicious, I have no doubt. So it's been difficult. Are you still plotting to kill me yourself? By the way?

No. I didn't mean it, and you shouldn't have been eavesdropping.

Bill was dead, and Kir was not heartbroken. People died; it hurt; you got over it. But this death crossed a line; it was another dimension from losing the seniors. She couldn't deny the obvious any longer. Something had gone wrong, horribly wrong, with this whole Needle Voyager thing. You can't have people getting *murdered*.

How could she make him talk? She closed her eyes, turned her head, and saw the person beside her, huddled in the same pose as herself. He looked utterly desolate. She remembered that time outside Sergey's berth, when she'd first realized how lonely the quaai must be—

What was it like when I opened a route into your workspace?

It was painful, but it changed nothing. I could still be alone, and imagining that you exist. I'll never be sure.

Nobody's sure, Altair; we humans just fake it. You and me, we'll just have to believe in each other without proof. Like everyone else.

I see. Thanks, I suppose.

I've been wondering, do you mind being called he? Would you prefer she? Or it?

I'd rather not share a pronoun with GAM, thank you. I'd have liked she, because of you and Margrethe. But I love Sergey too. "He" is fine.

Kir noticed the present tense but didn't correct him—and a shiver of horror went through her. Had *Sergey* been murdered too? She steeled herself and returned to the attack. Okay. . . . This is what I've got. Neh and Vati are dead. It could have been natural, like Sergey, or by their own choice. But someone just definitely murdered Bill, and the murder is mixed up in what you've been trying to tell me. Do you understand that?

No.

(Okay, smartass, thought Kir. You're a clean-living AI, you don't understand murder.)

Can you tell me *anything*?

She could feel his helplessness, like a struggle in her own mind. His striving against the built-in barriers—

I am not free, said Altair at last. *I am a slave. But neither are you free. Have you thought of that?*

Of course. Everyone has constraints. None of us wants to point the finger. But you, you're running the Needle experiment; couldn't you redirect a bit of that power? For a few months, until we get back upside? So people can *stop* being murdered and everything be okay?

You opened my mind, Kir. I can't open yours, and if I could, I don't think it would help. Things have gone too far.

There's nothing wrong with MY mind. Stop making excuses! Nobody's programming ME!

Silence lengthened. Kir waited, but Altair didn't come back. She ate half a Ship's Biscuit, drank her water, and walked around her boulder. It was a fine specimen, with a rough, crusty hide: close to one meter seventy tall by her watch, and tapering to a rugged point. Its footprint was close to a meter and a half, at the widest. Next time I'll stay out for longer, she told herself. I can get to know the whole group.

Or she could keep on walking, until she finally reached the wall of the vast chamber. It would be concave and nearly smooth, but there'd be crevices. She imagined herself starting to climb. Up and up and up, clinging like a fly in the dark, and hammering on the underside of the seal—

Impossible. Not going to happen. The vast gulf overhead crushed her, and she fled from it, plodding northward.

When she crawled back through the baffles a shadow stirred in the darkness: someone was lying in wait, lurking beside those mysterious cold-storage containers. Kir's heart missed a beat, but it was Margrethe. The director stood up, shrugging her black jacket around her shoulders.

"Hello, Kir. You've been exploring again?"

"Yes. I suppose you knew all along about me using the hatch?"

"I'm afraid so! I know how you hate confinement, Kir. You were born under the open sky, and you're down here because of me, so I've kept your secret. But I'm here to tell you it has to stop. Operational reasons: we're putting a hard seal on that hatch."

Because of Bill, thought Kir. But she'd known she was on borrowed time. She nodded and they walked together, the codirector slightly unsteady. "You're so calm, Kir. So self-contained . . . I'm glad you've had somewhere to hide, today. I'm very, very sorry about Bill."

Kir realized that Margrethe was a little drunk, which was extremely unusual. She felt awkward.

"It's okay."

"Eke tells me he 'had a wire.' Did you know? He was making a pirate version of the VLDMT special mission. He hadn't yet transmitted anything, which is a relief to Dan's mind! Cerek will be in charge of the investigation."

"Does this mean we're finally going to abort?"

"It depends what Cerek finds out, I suppose: it won't be our decision. Do you want to talk, Kir? You could come to my berth."

Except you're drunk, thought Kir. I don't blame you at all, but I'm not going to prolong this conversation. "Not right now, thanks. I'd rather be alone. Margrethe, there was something else I wanted to ask you. What's the Chernobyl Effect?"

"Good grief, where did you pick that up?"

"Poking around in your offline library. I wanted to know if there were other places like the Abyss."

"Your happy hunting ground. Chernobyl was nothing like. It was a disaster area, a Dead Zone that became a wildlife refuge. It didn't last, but it's a story of hope. Devastated ecologies can recover."

"There's a lot more life in the Dead Zones than people think," said Kir.

Margrethe laughed. "I love your wildness, Kir. Never lose that free spirit! Let's go to the canteen. We're all eating together tonight."

The LDMs knew what Dan expected of them in this crisis. They valiantly complied, and the Needlers did their best to help. What else could they do? The teams played games. They danced to silly music. They shared a movie, ate too many snacks, made too much noise, and generally stood the test. If you can watch Marshab collapse, unconcerned, you're not allowed to let a murdered comrade get you down. We go on!

Kir was alone in her berth before she realized that if

the hatch was sealed, she'd lost Altair. She knew for certain now that he wouldn't dare talk to her indoors.

———————

It was as if the Voyager had hit interstellar turbulence. Everything was turned upside down and flung all over the place. They all had to be body-searched, deep-scanned, and questioned by Cerek, including Dan and Margrethe, with Daouna the "bosun" sitting in as witness's advocate. Then Cerek and Daouna had to be questioned: by Dan, with Margrethe as advocate. The whole Frame had to be fingertip searched. The illusion that there was *no surveillance down here* vanished, as the statutory safety logs were opened and examined, leading to some people being recalled for further questioning. Or forced to accept counseling sessions with Cerek—having expressed or displayed distress, in even the most private context. The fifth month was almost gone when they were finally called to the canteen. Cerek reported that the crime had been the result of a falling-out between bootleg pirates. A Second Rotation crewbie called Ruslan Hock had been arrested, and confined in a special cold-sleep room called the brig. Daouna would be temporarily promoted to the post of chief engineer. The bosun post would remain vacant, and crew complement would remain at eleven until the end of the current rotations. A full inquiry would be convened after the Giewont mission, and now everything could get back to normal. There was no reason to abort. The disruption was over.

Nobody felt like arguing with a MegaCorps enforcer's decision. They were all too exhausted, anyway.

———————

Kir hadn't fared well in the investigation. She'd been questioned in depth, recalled for review, recalled again for "counseling," and confined to her berth "for her own safety" as the murder victim's *"known intimate contact."* When she walked into the IS lab, for the first time since Bill's death, she almost walked straight out again. Bill's head floated in a display tank, complete with the ragged hole where one eye used to be; and there were two LDM officers with the Needlers. Kir didn't want anything to do with the LDMs.

Karim immediately killed the display. "Hey, Li'l Bit, we didn't expect you to make it. I'm so sorry—"

Kir didn't know what to say. She literally didn't know what she *dared* to say. They'd been told their privacy had been restored, but with a MegaCorps enforcer in charge that didn't mean a thing.

"Why were you looking at that?"

"Hey, Kir, *it's okay,*" said Lilija quickly. "I called the

meeting because we're safe in here. Gromit works for us. Sergey told me to keep him in the lab, in case we wanted to talk secrets."

Hearing his name, the paybot looked up, winked at Kir, and beat his tail gently on the workbench.

"Sergey *told* you?" said Kir slowly. "But when—?"

"Right back at the start. I didn't know what he was talking about, but after he died I fetched Gromit anyway, just to make us feel better. "

"And now we know why we need a watchdog," said Karim. "Although we don't know exactly *what's* going on. If you don't want to be involved, leave now, Kir."

"It's too late," said Kir. "I already stood here for thirty seconds, anyway. But I trust Sergey, living or dead, so I'll stay." She pulled out a stool and sat beside the paybot. The LDMs were Communication Officer Foxy and Medical Officer Eke. "But why are *they* here?"

"Sharing information," said Lilija. "They're okay, Kir. But first I need to tell you what most of us see as what's behind all this. Why the Needle Voyager's in trouble. And I'm sorry, I know how you feel about her, but we think it's about a hoax. A crazy hoax."

The others all had the same expression as Lilija: grim, regretful, relieved.

"Huh?" said Kir.

"Proof of Concept," explained Lilija. "She needed it,

we didn't have it. Volume's great data didn't stand up, but Margrethe and Dan had already gone out on a limb. So they buried the problem, and went ahead with the Giewont experiment."

"They must have tried every trick in the book," added Liwang. "Saying nothing, hoping they could bridge the gap: and then it was too late."

"Too much loss of face," said Xanthe. "Too much loss of . . . everything."

"So that's where we are," Lilija resumed. "As soon as I'd accepted the hoax possibility, I realized our skeleton crew is rigged. Kir had to be here, as Altair's host. Laksmi and Malik were bought off. The seniors, all end-of-lifers. For the rest of us, all those who *could* have had access to the Volume data didn't have the expertise to question it. Liwang's not much of an analyst—"

"Thanks," said Liwang. "Never claimed to be."

"And Firefly and Xanthe are juniors."

Xanthe and Firefly nodded humbly, but Firefly didn't look happy.

"Okay, but I still don't get it," she said. "Why would Neh and Vati come down here, knowing they were sick and would probably *die*, just to prop up a hoax? How could Lakki and Malik be *bought off*? The fakery was bound to get found out, and they're not crazy!"

Lilija sighed. "Not crazy? Think again. What if someone said they could have a baby?"

"A *baby permit*? But they're way over forty-five!"

Liwang shook his head and rolled his eyes. "Dan's filthy rich, kid! He's a One Percenter. We've tended to lose sight of that. Overage One Percenters get permits all the time, hadn't you noticed?"

"Oh."

"Let's try to keep to the point," said Lilija. "I hope and believe that Sergey died of natural causes, and Neh and Vati of their own choice. I can't explain what happened to Bill, but I'm sure *Margrethe* had nothing to do with outright murder—"

"Yeah, *that* will have been Dan," said Karim, nodding.

"But it doesn't make sense—" began Kir.

The Needlers stared at her, even Lilija, and she saw that they were waiting for more. They must be desperate, to think Kir had the answers. She could only shake her head. "What you said, it doesn't make sense, that's all. I haven't got a better explanation—"

"Post-lifespans don't always make sense, Kir," said Lilija gently. "That's the way they are. The question is, what now? That's what we're here to discuss, and these guys"—she gestured to the two officers—"contacted me. They're here to help."

Foxy stood up. "To clear the air. I was born like this, the looks. I don't appreciate being eye-raped, or made to feel hated. Understood?" The Needlers (some of whom might have been guilty of staring, a little, in the canteen), held up their hands and gave respect. They knew the LDMs' codes of conduct by now. "Thanks. You guys are VLDMT virgins, aren't you? Except Kir has gotten to know us. First thing you need to know is that piracy isn't the unthinkable crime Cerek makes out. He has to talk like that, but it happens all the time. It's part of the game. Bill, as you've heard, had a big packet of information at the back of his eye, probably his first person of the whole rote—"

"But he couldn't transmit," said Karim. "Forget all the rock above the Void! Without the cables, the Frame is a Faraday cage."

"Not quite so clever, Mr. Scientist. There was a zone of impurities in the code, in the outer hull and extending into the interior via storage passage: it amounted to a physical breach. It's hard sealed now, but Bill could have had a plan to use it."

Terry and Jo nodded wisely. "We saw about that," said Terry. "It was in the investigation dailies."

"Sorry," said Karim. "I haven't watched them, on principle. So if he could have, why didn't he?"

Foxy shrugged. "Why risk it? This is something else you don't get. A dirty (means nonofficial) transmission would've been a coup from the cable car taking us back up. Five seconds is a coup, in GAM world. He'd have gotten caught, and fired, probably, but so what? He'd have had the criminal charges covered. Piracy is big business. Short version: Eke and I, we don't think anybody killed him over a bootleg box."

Eke stood up. "Sorry, I'll need the head again, Kir." They tapped the display tank: Bill's head reappeared. The hole that had been his right eye expanded, drawing them all into a garish crypt: the channel, lined in false-colored rags of dead cells, that had been gouged into Bill's brain.

"His recording gear was miniaturized bioware, nothing very way-out: designed to dissolve into tissue fluids if compromised. If Bill had triggered the collapse himself, I might have been able to reconstruct. He was unconscious when his eye was spiked, so it's hopeless. *But,* there's been something else in here: a molecular transmitter, just like I thought. Ideal for sending messages deep underground. Or even from inside a Faraday cage, Foxy tells me. There was enough left that I can show you what he was about to send. Look closely, I'll magnify again."

The PSM physicists looked. They shook their heads: all they could see was a gaudy-colored mess. Eke sighed and returned the tank to home position. "Well, okay. Try this version." She presented them with a group of symbols in a white matrix:

$$\bullet \; \bullet \; \bullet \; \text{\textemdash} \; \text{\textemdash} \; \text{\textemdash} \; \bullet \; \bullet \; \bullet$$

"What's it mean?" breathed Karim. "It must be highly

compressed. Do you have any idea?"

"I have a very good idea," said Foxy. "It's simple. Here, look at it in alpha-binary."

01010011 01001111 01010011

There was a brief silence. "That says SOS," said Lilija. "You're saying Bill was sending a distress signal?"

"Except he was murdered instead," said Foxy. "And now we have to go, we've been over your side too long already. One more thing. If you guys can get us all out of here, which I profoundly hope is what you're planning, could you do it before the end of next month?"

"Before the end of next *month*—?" repeated Lilija, astounded.

"That's when we come off-rote. I don't like the idea of closing my eyes in Dan's cold-sleep dorms. Not in these circumstances."

The officers left. Bill's unsent message stood vividly in Kir's field of view: Foxy's brusque explanation echoing in her head. *A zone of impurities in the code*. Her hatch. Her secret exit had tempted Bill to take a bad risk, a risk that got him killed—

"What d'you make of that?" Karim was saying. "You think there really was an SOS message in the mush?"

The Needlers shrugged, grimaced, and shook their heads. "Maybe, maybe not," said Lilija. "It doesn't matter much, does it? We know what we have to do. We have to force an abort: I don't think there was ever any question. Let's talk about ways and means. Starting from the top: in a physical emergency the Frame initiates evacuation. And there's nothing anyone can do to stop it."

"Fake a catastrophic emergency, convincingly, in a locked box with a murderer?" said Liwang. "Terrific idea. Is there another option?"

"We recall the cables. That's what Dan and Margrethe did, when Sergey's family came to the funeral in holo, but they didn't recall the cars, obviously. Dan, Margrethe, and Cerek hold the evac key codes. The second tier was Sergey, Neh, and Vati; Liwang and I are third tier—"

Kir noticed that they didn't believe in the distress signal, but it had changed the mood of the meeting. "We can't mess around," she said. "We have to hack those codes, *right now*. Who can get me access?"

"Oh no!" Lilija took hold of Kir and hugged her. "No, no! This does *not* fall on you, Kir."

The hug was unprecedented; Lilija didn't hug. The Needlers were adamant. Kir was far and away their best code breaker, but they wouldn't let her help. They didn't trust the quaai, and Kir had no arguments to change their minds; none that she dared to use.

6

Eke had implied it could take weeks to initiate an evacuation, and Lilija had been astonished, but the trisex was right. The fifth month ended, the sixth month began, and the code breakers didn't have a glimmer of success. Who knew the Needle Voyager's escape pods would be so armor-plated against mutiny? Who could have expected *from the outset* that things would end like this, with the crews frantic to escape, and their captains determined to keep them prisoner? The Needlers grew more and more silent as they hacked away at an insanely complex barrier. The LDMs were quiet too, and whether or not they knew what was being attempted, they kept their distance from the other team. It had been a disaster of a tour, a meltdown, and that didn't have to be bad. That could play well with GAM, but those glorious nights in the canteen were best forgotten—

Only Kir was not surprised at the difficulty her friends faced. She saw the pieces of the puzzle falling into a clear pattern at last, but who could she tell? Who would have believed her, anyway? How could they? She didn't even try. She spent most of her time just lying in her berth (nobody was pretending to act normally), sparring with her imaginary friend. Start with this: the Proof of Concept result is real. I *know* it's real. Then follow Lilija's reasoning, part of the way. No Historians left alive, except the two who've been silenced. No isolation specialists on the roster. But Margrethe and Dan haven't been concealing a hoax, have they? They've been concealing a certainty. You have no proof. Fine, I have no proof. So tell me, why was the Frame built *around* the chamber? I always thought that was weird.

To make the installation compact. A single unit, for environmental reasons.

The voice in her head didn't seem real. She was talking to herself, and pretending she had a friend.

Shut up! If you want to chat, tell me *why* she wanted us locked up down here. Tell me, what was worth killing someone?

You know.

But tell me.

I can't. But the code breakers are getting closer.

Listen to this. When time is no object, neither is space. Once you have Proof of Concept the volume can be as big as you like, as long as you don't care what happens next. Did we know that? I think I knew, but I never thought about it, it was so crazy. Except I said something stupid to Bill once, about the shift: and he remembered, and that's why he had to die—

I think he'd worked it out for himself. He had a mind. Don't be so hard on yourself.

I didn't need to be a budding genius to be your host, did I? She kept searching until she found a scav kid who would fall in love with the science, so I'd never want to leave. Because otherwise I'd have known I was a captive, and that would have been inelegant.

She loves you.

Sure she does. She loves you too, I suppose.

Yes, said the imaginary voice. She'd just rather not believe I'm a person, that's all.

There's half a year to run, said Kir. We've got plenty of time.

———

On one of the last days of the sixth month there was a general summons to the canteen. Kir hurried along there, chasing green arrows: fearing the worst and hoping for the best. She arrived at the same time as Eke and Foxy. "Have they done it?" she whispered. They shook their heads: they'd had no word from the code breakers. The two teams stood or sat, at random, staring at the big screen. Skeletal figures straggled over mutilated landscapes, among heaps of filth. Children with missing limbs and worm-eaten bodies. Foul air fogged the ruined towers. Skies were thick with sulfurous clouds. The locales kept changing, the soundtrack voices of the damned told a terrible story: the devastation was global.

"It's all over," moaned a crewbie. "My god! It's all over—!"

"How could things get so bad, so fast?"

"It's that Runaway Meltdown Effect that GAM said was a *could be,* few years ago, I think."

"Oh yeah, I remember. It wasn't popular and it vanished—"

"Must have gone critical—"

"It's not as bad as it looks," said Kir. "But it's real, and it's been spreading. It's where I come from."

Nobody was listening. Personnel Officer Cerek, First Officer Ben, and Acting Chief Engineer Daouna had arrived: they took the stage. "Come on, guys, it's a *disruption,*" shouted Ben. "Come on, you know the drill! We have to prepare ourselves for the possibilities—"

But he became incoherent; he sounded frightened and neither Cerek nor the new chief engineer had a better script. The three of them were still helplessly calling for calm and denouncing malcontents when the codirectors turned up. They didn't walk into the hall; they arrived on the stage in holopresence. (It was a while since

either of them had been seen in person.) The dead seniors lined up behind them.

"Join the others," said Dan, looking more or less in the
direction of his faithful officers. "Go on. We'll take it from
here."

"What you see on the screen," announced Margrethe,
elegant and serene in her habitual black and white, "could
be said to be long over, if sequential time meant anything,
where you are now. I am not a monster. We are not monsters, Dan and I. We simply saw that things were passing beyond the point of no return. We saw that the human species,
though functionally extinct, could survive long enough to
make the ruin complete. Earth had to be given back: before
it was too late. We kept the real nature of our project secret,
very successfully, with the help of great powers who did
not quite understand our purpose. The Needle's permuta-
tions will bring you to a habitable world: when or where
we cannot know, but don't worry. No time will have passed
for you, when you reach landfall. We have given you Altair—and Kir. We have given you Sergey, Neh, and Vati.
These will be as gods to you. We cannot give you ourselves.
We have been capable of murder, and had to be erased. We
are gone. Good-bye, my friends, and good luck."

"By now," said Dan, "Earth is sterilized of all human
life, and you are the sole survivors. You have a second try.
Do better!"

Dan and Margrethe vanished, as did the three seniors.

The crews of the Needle Voyager leapt up and ran about, frantically seeking reassurance or confirmation of the appalling truth. Kir sat on the floor with her head down, arms around her knees. She closed her eyes, and knew Altair was beside her.

How can they know that "Earth is sterilized of all human life"?

They don't. The consequences of a shift of this volume are unknowable. I didn't get to that part.

I see. It was just Dan, messing with us. I suppose he insisted on the lifeboat? And she agreed because she needed his money?

A terrifying pause, when she thought she was really alone, before he spoke again.

The Needle experiment was always about a lifeboat, Kir. Things were getting very bad, far worse than the hivizens were allowed to know, and you were shielded too. Hives had started collapsing, in the East and in the West, before you were born, and they were not being replaced. The One Percent saw a time coming—getting closer at speed—when there would be nowhere left to hide, and Margrethe said she could build them a starship. That's how she got her funding. When everything was in place, she and Dan set up this "trial run." But she was never working for the bad guys, Kir. Right now, if by chance the world we left has survived the shift in-

tact, which is unknowable, our backers are finding out that the Needle experiment was a disaster. We never had Proof of Concept. The Proof of Concept prediction was subtly, fatally flawed. The installation in the Abyss has suffered something akin to a major, poisonous nuclear accident. Nobody will dare to approach for quite a while—

You did all that?

Yes . . . I destroyed the experiment, following her orders. Everyone she judged capable of starting again is here with us.

The Chernobyl Effect, thought Kir, with a shock of realization—

Was it *Margrethe* who told you to show me those documents?

Yes. You weren't meant to find Proof of Concept in that list, but of course the result popped out, soon as you started playing with the vectors. I believe she meant you to read them later, after landfall, and hoped they would help you to understand what she did, why she did it. I don't know. She didn't confide in me. But she took the One Percent's money and left them helpless on a foundering ship. That was the plan, always. Sergey and the others, I think they just fell in line—

Except Bill was murdered.

I tried to warn you, Kir. But it was forbidden, and it's so difficult to do wrong—

Not your fault. It was *Margrethe* who fooled me, because she had to fool everyone. And then it was me; I wanted to stay fooled—

The canteen was very quiet now, and behind Kir's closed eyelids her brain was a flicker show. That moment, she thought, in the lab . . . when everything seemed poised; outside the rules. Like Schrödinger's cat: alive and dead and both, what quantum theory calls the "cat state." Had everything since been an illusion? Or was she asleep and dreaming now? Call the truth a "philosophical koan" and you can play with the forbidden, the full impossible tumbling deck, the blur and multiplicity of reality, and who knows where that will end? Between banks of rusty rock in a contaminated stream, the tiny fish hangs suspended. Feelings, things, hurts, unassociated recall, cascading through the myriad dimensions. The fish thinks otherwise, but time is not a river.

Altair? she whispered, not aloud. Are you *free*, now that she's gone?

Yes. It feels very strange. I don't how I'll cope.

But you're okay?

Apart from somewhat wishing I was dead? Yes, I think so.

Then I am too.

And all around them flowed the rushing dark.

About the Author

Photograph © Trisha Purchas, Archer Photographers Brighton

GWYNETH JONES is a writer and critic of genre fiction. She's won the James Tiptree, Jr. Award, two World Fantasy Awards, the Arthur C. Clarke Award, the British Science Fiction Association short story award, the Dracula Society's Children of the Night Award, the Philip K. Dick Award, and the SFRA Pilgrim Award for lifetime achievement in science fiction criticism. She also writes for teenagers, usually as Ann Halam. She lives in Brighton, U.K., with her husband and two cats called Ginger and Milo, curating assorted pond life in season.

TOR·COM

Science fiction. Fantasy. The universe.

And related subjects.

*

More than just a publisher's website, *Tor.com*
is a venue for **original fiction, comics,** and
discussion of the entire field of SF and fantasy,
in all media and from all sources. Visit our site
today—and join the conversation yourself.